THEY CAME TO DURANGO

Quint Burgess—His dreams and hopes were battered by the West, but from deep inside he found a reserve of strength that could stand up to any challenge.

Mountain Laurel—With the medical training of her Quaker physician father and the traditional Indian secrets learned from her Ute mother's tribe, she was a woman with the power to heal and the courage to overcome the hatred she faced as a half-breed.

Ned Purvis and Custer Vance—Human dregs from the mining camp, they preyed on innocent travellers and looked to this Durango stage to be their personal gold-strike.

Sadie Goode—Her quick-thinking and rapid action saved the passengers once, but her driving greed could expose them to a deadlier fate.

The Stagecoach Series
Ask your bookseller for the books you have missed

STAGECOACH STATION 17:

DURANGO

Hank Mitchum

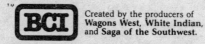

Created by the producers of
Wagons West, White Indian,
and **Saga of the Southwest.**

Chairman of the Board: Lyle Kenyon Engel

BANTAM BOOKS
TORONTO • NEW YORK • LONDON • SYDNEY • AUCKLAND

STAGECOACH STATION 17: DURANGO

*A Bantam Book / published by arrangement with
Book Creations, Inc.*

*Produced by Book Creations, Inc.
Chairman of the Board: Lyle Kenyon Engel*

Bantam edition / April 1985

ISBN 0-553-24811-1

Published simultaneously in the United States and Canada

---

*Bantam Books are published by Bantam Books, Inc. Its trademark,
consisting of the words "Bantam Books" and the portrayal of a
rooster, is Registered in U.S. Patent and Trademark Office and in
other countries. Marca Registrada. Bantam Books, Inc., 666 Fifth
Avenue, New York, New York 10103.*

PRINTED IN THE UNITED STATES OF AMERICA

O   0 9 8 7 6 5 4 3 2 1

STAGECOACH STATION 17:

DURANGO

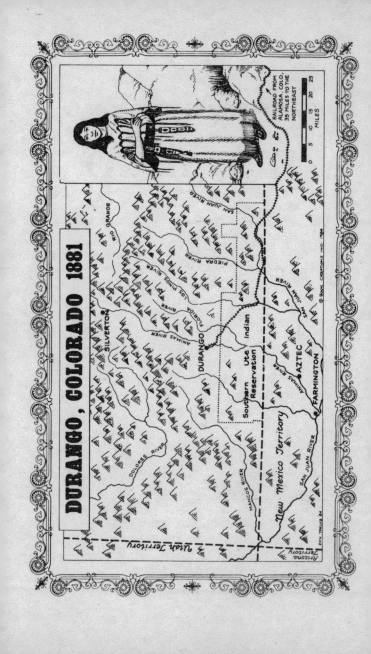

DURANGO, COLORADO 1881

RAILROAD FROM
ALAMOSA, COLO.
35 MILES TO THE
NORTHEAST

0 5 10 15 20 25
MILES

© BOOK CREATIONS INC. 1966

RIO GRANDE

SILVERTON

PIEDRA RIVER

SAN JUAN RIVER

LOS PINOS RIVER

FLORIDA RIVER

ANIMAS RIVER

DURANGO

Southern Ute Indian Reservation

AZTEC

ANIMAS RIVER

JUAN RIVER

FARMINGTON

New Mexico Territory

DOLORES RIVER

MANCOS RIVER

SAN JUAN RIVER

Utah Territory

Arizona Territory

RON TRACY 84

Chapter One

The crisp morning wind poured across the arid table-land of northern New Mexico Territory, each wave leaving the sparse gray grass shivering in its wake. The early autumn whirlwind rolled relentlessly toward the distant wall that was the southern Colorado Rockies, sweeping across a land unbroken by trees, boulders, or bushes.

Across the wide expanse sat but a single obstacle to its passage, a cluster of crude buildings—little more than weather-ravaged boards and caked mud chinking—that shuddered and groaned as they clung like so many dried barnacles to the barren earth. And as the wind fought its way between the buildings and through gaps in the boards, it transformed the single street of the town into a blinding dustbowl.

A large black dog, tail down and nose to the ground, explored the dusty, deserted street of Farmington. He sniffed at the entrance hole where a tiny wild animal had sought shelter under the sagging porch of the equally dilapidated New Mexico Grand Hotel. For a moment the dog considered trying to squeeze his large frame through the insubstantial opening, then he thought better of it and dashed across the street, yelping in surprise as a bouncing mass of tumbleweed whipped across his path.

The dog jumped up onto the walkway in front of

Farmington's only general store and lifted his head to eye the assorted wonders behind the large-pane window: bolts of calico cloth sharing a counter with jars of multicolored horehound mint sticks; a row of red and green single-wheeled barrows stenciled with the words Ames Plow Co. of Boston; a curiously wooden-looking, faceless woman regally draped in a lavender shirtwaist dress with a lace-trimmed parasol dangling from her dainty yet rigid wrist.

After a moment the dog's attention wandered, and he turned to look up and down the street in search of new avenues of adventure. He had just chosen his destination and was about to step off the walkway into the whirlwind when a furious thunderclap exploded directly overhead, followed by a series of bone-jarring bangs. As if propelled by a cannonblast, the dog leaped out into the street and was gone, caught up in the northward rush of windblown dirt and debris. Behind him, the sign outside Grady's Nickel Emporium swung wildly from a single chain, repeatedly crashing against the upright posts of the walkway overhang as its broken second chain furiously whipped the clapboard storefront.

Few citizens as yet dared venture outside on this October morning. They knew that as the sun rose higher, the winds would soften and the choking dust would settle back to the ground.

One man whose business could not await the stilling of the wind was Quint Burgess. Tall and lean with dark brown hair and drooping mustache, he struck an imposing figure in his gray-felt plainsman's hat and knee-length bearskin coat as he opened the door of a small free-standing adobe building and stepped out into the street. The wooden handle of a Bowie knife rested in easy reach of his right hand inside the neck of his high-topped boot, while his left hand carried a canvas sack bearing the words U.S. Mail.

Squinting his steel-blue eyes as he tossed the sack

over his shoulder, Quint faced the wind and headed toward a barn fifty feet away, where an imposing vehicle stood waiting to be hitched up and hauled off into the dust storm. The four-wheeled behemoth was a Concord stage-coach, twenty-five hundred pounds of hickory, iron, and leather, seating up to nine passengers inside, but capable of bearing a full load of twenty-one when the occasion demanded.

Quint tossed the mail sack up into the driver's boot, then walked around to the left side of the coach to make sure the carriage door was securely latched. He ran a hand over the green basswood door panel, with its faded yet still-majestic depiction of the Rocky Mountains painted in oils. Though winter storms and dry summer winds had long since dulled the sheen of the lacquered woodwork, this was still a sturdy vehicle worthy of the Concord's long reputation as the most comfortable and dependable form of transportation west of the Mississippi—a reputation rapidly being eclipsed by that of the railroad.

This particular Concord was the flagship vehicle of the stage line that shuttled passengers between Santa Fe, two hundred miles to the southeast, and Durango, Colorado, fifty miles to the north. And at thirty-three, Quint Burgess was the line's foremost driver, handling the Farmington-Durango leg of the run. The aging feeder line had formerly been known as the Farmington Stage Line, and for many years it had served a small but loyal clientele between Santa Fe and Farmington. But when the Denver and Rio Grande Railroad had completed their narrow-gauge run from Alamosa, Colorado, through Toltec Gorge and cre-ated the town of Durango in the previous year of 1880, the stage line had extended its service, had bought additional equipment, and with great fanfare and high hopes had rechristened itself the Durango Overland Stage Line.

Such early optimism proved far from warranted, and the line now found itself overextended and understaffed, forced increasingly to pay its remaining employees with hollow promises and prayers. Yet a spirit of camaraderie and pride prevailed among the drivers, stockmen, and stationmasters—men who appreciated the role they had played in taming the West.

As Quint turned toward the horse barn, he heard the muffled slam of a door and then saw two huddled figures heading toward him through the swirling dust storm. They were coming from the Grand Hotel, and from the way the man was weighed down with baggage, Quint had no doubt they were the first of this morning's passengers. The man wore a brown derby and had the collar of his leather jacket pulled up high around his face, and it was not until he was within a few yards that Quint realized he was black. The woman, carrying a single large carpetbag, walked several steps behind, the heavy fur-trimmed hood of her russet wool coat concealing her features and skin color.

"Station?" the black man shouted in an effort to be heard above the whirlwind, a nod of his head indicating the nearby adobe structure.

"Yes, that's it," Quint replied, then reached for one of the bags. "I'll stow these things for you."

Quint took the bag around to the rear luggage boot, and the man followed. The woman had reached them now, and she stood watching patiently as Quint opened the leather skirt that covered the boot, loaded each bag inside, and covered it over again. Then he stepped over to where she was standing and motioned toward the carpetbag in her hand.

"Shall I load that, ma'am, or would you like it under your seat?"

The woman reached up with her free hand and pulled her hood back slightly. Even through the dusty haze, Quint could see how her amber eyes sparkled, and her skin was as soft and pale as a child's. Though she was no longer young—Quint guessed her to be a few years older than himself—her smooth features evinced a youthfulness that had been carefully shielded from time, like a lovingly preserved porcelain doll.

"Yes, I'd like it with me," she whispered, her words barely perceptible in the stiffening breeze. "May I wait inside the carriage?"

"Of course." Quint opened the coach door and offered his hand.

The woman handed her carpetbag to her companion, accepted Quint's hand, lifted the hem of her skirt, and stepped up onto the iron stair that was suspended from the side of the coach. In a moment she had taken a seat with her back to the front of the stage—where the effects of dust or rain would be least. Then she leaned forward to the open doorway.

"Tom, would you take care of our tickets?" she asked her companion as he placed the carpetbag on the floor in front of her. She reached into a small purse that dangled from her wrist and handed him several gold coins. "This should cover our fare."

"Yes, Miss Williman," he replied, pocketing the coins and heading for the stage office.

Rather than leaning back in her seat, the woman sat looking at Quint as he closed the coach door. "You *are* the driver, aren't you?" she asked as she pulled off her hood, revealing long red hair tied to one side with a yellow ribbon.

"Yes. Quint Burgess, ma'am. Pleased to meet you."

"And I'm Rebecca Williman, on my way to Durango." She smiled as she reached through the open window and offered Quint her hand.

He shook it gently, then nodded politely and muttered, "I must see to the horses, Miss Williman."

"Rebecca. It's Rebecca."

"Yes," he replied, trying not to smile sheepishly as

he backed from the coach, turned around, and headed quickly to the barn.

Rebecca Williman watched Quint until he disappeared through the barn door. Then she leaned back against the padded leather seat and sighed. Her doctor had insisted that this trip to Durango was just what she needed to overcome her grief at her father's recent death, but somehow nothing seemed to interest her anymore—not even that tall, good-looking stage driver in the long fur coat.

Tom Kennedy stepped into the adobe building, shut the door tightly against the wind, and turned to survey the dingy office. As he pulled off his battered derby with his right hand and slapped it against his thigh to remove the dust, his left hand first rubbed his eyes, then his completely bald scalp. Though he was neither tall nor imposing in stature, his compact frame gave an impression of great strength and agility, and even his smallest movements held the grace of a mountain lion.

Noticing a boy about ten years old sitting by himself on a bench against the wall, Kennedy broke into a broad smile, as he always did around children. He arched his bushy black eyebrows and made a friendly face, his large brown eyes wide open and sparkling. But the lad's silent, almost hollow expression remained unchanged, as if he were looking through the black stranger. Kennedy recalled the many adults who had reacted to him in the same manner and who taught their children the subtle and insidious art. In many ways Kennedy found this more painful, more cruel, than the blatant prejudice of those many others who wore their venomous hatred like a badge of pride.

But Kennedy sensed something different about this sandy-haired child—something missing. The boy's empty expression did not seem to mask an underlying nervousness or guilt, like the facades of his elders. And as Kennedy walked away from the door and started toward the counter, he realized that the lad was not merely looking through one black man, he was looking through the entire world around him. It was as if the boy's body were sitting on the bench, while his spirit had withdrawn to a distant place and time.

"Can I help you, mister?"

The thin, high-pitched voice pulled Kennedy out of his reverie, and he turned from the boy on the bench to see a young clerk, no more than fourteen years old, staring up at him from the other side of the counter. Despite his youth, the clerk seemed to take his job quite seriously. He wore a green eyeshade, which served mostly to hold back his auburn bangs, and his watery-blue eyes were squinted into a studied facsimile of a businesslike expression.

"Uh, yes, I came about a ticket," Kennedy began, then glanced back at the boy on the bench. The strange child's delicate features remained unchanged—unmoved.

"Don't mind him," the clerk said. "That's Lucas Burgess, the stage driver's boy. He don't mean no harm." The clerk hooked his thumbs on his striped gray vest and leaned toward Kennedy. With a conspiratorial gleam in his eyes, he tapped the side of his forehead and whispered, "He ain't all there, if you get my meaning."

"Yes," the black man muttered, only half listening. "Yes, I see."

"Going to Durango, I presume."

Kennedy turned completely to the counter now. He lifted a couple of the gold coins from his pocket and placed them in front of the young clerk. "Yes, and there are two of us. Two for Durango."

"That'll be twenty dollars even," the clerk explained, picking up the pair of ten-dollar gold pieces. "But it's another two dollars each if you'd like food."

"How many meals?"

"We send lunch in the coach, and there's a late-afternoon dinner at the Ute reservation way station. But don't worry about the reservation; they serve up real American food, not Indian dog meat. At breakfast you'll be in Durango, and you'll have to buy your own.''

"Yes, we'd like meals,'' Kennedy replied as he counted out the required coins and tossed them over.

Just then the front door of the stage office was yanked open, and a petite woman in a long blue cloak hurried into the room, followed closely by an equally slight young man, who carried a carpetbag in each hand and an additional one under each arm. With a grunt of relief, the fellow carelessly dropped the four bags to the plank floor.

As the man removed his narrow-brimmed hat and the woman her hood, Kennedy saw that their hair was an identical flaxen yellow, hers long and straight and his in tight little ringlets. And even from his distance across the room, Kennedy noted that the sky blue of their eyes was also a perfect match. He might have taken them for brother and sister if the woman had not just then leaned over, kissed the fellow lovingly on the cheek, and murmured, ''I hope that wasn't too heavy, Stephen, dear,'' to which he replied, "Not at all, Mrs. Davis.'' They were obviously husband and wife, and from their age—Kennedy guessed they could not be a day over twenty—he was convinced they were newly married.

"Ah, you over there,'' the blond man suddenly called in a thick southern accent as he looked toward the counter and beckoned with his right hand. ''You, boy, come see to these bags.''

There was something annoyingly superior in the fellow's tone that sent an involuntary shudder through Kennedy. He felt sorry for the boy clerk, whose job it was to see to his customer's every need, and he turned to give the youth a sympathetic smile. But as he glanced back at the counter, he discovered there was nobody there; the clerk had disappeared into the back office.

"*Boy,* I asked you to do something for me,'' the

southerner repeated, his voice taking on a biting edge and his hand now clearly indicating Tom Kennedy.

"Boy?" the black man repeated incredulously. "Me? Your boy? I'm easily twice your age, *sonny*." He kept a firm smile planted on his face as he tried to contain his emotions, knowing how easily they could transform into rage.

The southerner's hands clenched into fists, and his eyes flashed arrogantly. He began to take a step toward Kennedy, but his visibly uncomfortable wife yanked at the sleeve of his brown, fur-lined overcoat, pleading, "Stephen, dear, this isn't Georgia."

Stephen slowly relaxed his hands and breathed deeply, as if weighing the advisability of pursuing the matter with such a formidable stranger—a black man obviously unaccustomed to conforming to his rightful place in society. "Damn western Yankees," he finally muttered. "There's no sense of propriety out here."

The southerner turned back toward his luggage, and in so doing he noticed Lucas Burgess sitting by himself on one of the benches. A new thought struck him, and he sang out, "Hey, young fellow, how about a hand carrying these bags to the stage?"

This time Lucas reacted by turning his head a little and staring in the direction of the voice. His head tilted slightly and his soft gray eyes narrowed, as if the thickly accented words were a curious melody he was trying to discern.

When Lucas made no further reaction, Stephen tried again. "Did you hear me? Tote these bags and there might be a penny in it for you."

At that moment the young clerk emerged from the back office and saw the Davises, his eyes brightening as he recognized the young southern couple, who had arrived on the previous stage and had stayed over in Farmington.

"Never mind him, Mr. Davis," the clerk called out as he hurried around the counter. "I'll see to your things."

"Thanks, uhh, William. That *is* your name, isn't it?" Stephen asked as the clerk wedged the two smallest bags under his arms and reached for the handles of the larger ones.

Beaming with pride at having been remembered, the clerk replied, "Yes, that's right, Mr. Davis. And good morning to you, ma'am," he added, nodding at the southerner's pretty wife. "Did you enjoy your stay in Farmington?"

"Oh, yes," the young woman said with a noticeable lack of conviction. "After that long ride from Santa Fe, I just couldn't have gone on to Durango on the last stage. You were most kind to suggest the hotel."

"Glad to be of service, ma'am." The youth straightened up, lifted the bags off the floor, and started toward the door.

As the clerk fumbled with the luggage, trying to free a few fingers to open the door, the woman quickly nudged her husband and gave him a knowing look. As if suddenly remembering an earlier conversation, Stephen returned her expression and hurried quickly to the door.

"Let me open that for you," he said, grasping the doorknob with one hand while his other hand reached inside his coat and removed a small gold coin. "And this is for you, William. Mrs. Davis and I appreciate your thoughtfulness." He slipped the coin into the young clerk's vest pocket.

"Why, th-thank you," William stammered, his pale cheeks glowing a ruddy red.

Stephen started to push the door open into the wind, then paused to ask, "Have you any idea how soon we'll be leaving?"

"We're due to pull out in five minutes, Mr. Davis, sir."

The clerk pushed through the half-open door and stepped out onto the walkway, then turned to look in at the passengers. Though the windstorm was lessening, it framed him in a swirl of dust and set his vest lapels flapping.

"We're just waiting on two final passengers," he called, his reedy voice barely distinguishable from the wind. "But if they're not here in ten minutes, we ride without them. They delivered their bags and bought their tickets last night. Couple by the name of Goode."

Joseph Grady stood precariously on the top rung of an A-frame ladder on the windswept walkway in front of his store. With one hand pressed up against the overhang to balance himself, he lifted the dangling end of the store sign and tried to reattach it to its chain.

Suddenly the elderly storekeeper felt something grab hold of his right ankle, and it so startled him that he let go of the sign. As it fell and swung wildly from the single chain, it crashed into his side, almost knocking him from the ladder, and he had to grab hold of one of the walkway posts to keep from falling. His feet dancing to keep their purchase atop the ladder, he slowly regained his balance and pushed himself back away from the upright post, though he still held tight to the beam.

Again Grady felt something pulling at his ankle, and he summoned the courage to look down. Below, a short, heavyset, middle-aged woman was protecting her hair with one hand while anxiously tugging at his pant leg with the other. Beside her was a gaunt, equally short man with narrow wire-rim glasses, an apologetic look on his face.

"Excuse me, mister, but are you open yet?" the woman inquired in a harsh, guttural voice as she picked up the large handbag she had set down on the walkway. "Sorry to be a bother, but we've supplies to get and a stage to catch."

Steadying the sign with one hand, Grady cautiously

climbed down the ladder and forced a thin smile. "Why, yes, of course. Welcome to Grady's Nickel Emporium. Won't you come in?"

He quickly folded the ladder and laid it down on the walkway against the storefront. As he swung open the door, it struck a small, spring-mounted bell, which gaily announced their entrance. Grady ushered the couple inside, then removed his overcoat and placed it on a chair beside the door. He brushed off his brown waistcoat, ran his hand across his long white hair, and asked, "May I be of service to you?"

The woman loosened her coat, revealing a more-than-robust figure barely contained in a gaudy lime-green dress, its plunging neckline trimmed with generous folds of lace that converged and parted with each breath. She turned to the storekeeper and was about to speak, but then her attention was distracted by some movement of her companion, who was busily fingering the lavender gown on a mannequin in the window.

"Now, Arvis," she chided him, "don't be making a pest of yourself. Why don't you go look around the store, while I see to business with this nice gentleman." As she said the word "gentleman," she turned back to Grady and gave him a broad, suggestive smile.

Arvis wandered off toward the back of the store, muttering, "Whatever you say, my dear," but no one heard him. The woman was fastidiously fluffing the lace at her chest, and Joseph Grady was trying to appear nonchalant, his eyes narrowing every time she inhaled.

The woman stepped closer to the storekeeper, until they were almost touching, and whispered, "If you don't mind my saying so, Grady's Nickel Emporium is almost as impressive as its owner."

Grady could see that this middle-aged coquette was far from beautiful—her features were as harsh as her voice, and her dull brown hair was drawn up in a tight, severe bun. But her flattery had its effect, and with a gleam in his eye the elderly man rephrased his earlier inquiry: "And how may I be of service to you, ma'am?"

The woman returned his knowing smile. "We need some medicinal supplies for our stage journey. They're for my husband—he's such a bother. He claims he's got consumption, but the doctors say it's his imagination. He promised to take me for a couple of weeks to Santa Fe, but as soon as we arrived he started complaining about his health, and we had to turn right around and head back for Durango."

The storekeeper looked over at Arvis, who was examining the merchandise along the back wall of the store. "I must admit he doesn't look too healthy."

"Oh, forget about him." She placed her hand on Grady's forearm to regain his full attention. "Now, didn't you offer me your service?"

The storekeeper turned back to the woman and gently rested his hand on hers, holding it slightly longer than propriety allowed. Then he backed away and walked around the counter. "What can I get you?"

"Two bottles of whiskey, to start with. I tell Arvis to take it for medicinal purposes, but it's really to put him to sleep so he will keep from pestering me."

Grady turned around, removed two bottles from one of the shelves along the wall, and set them on the counter. As the woman opened her large handbag and placed them inside, he asked, "Is there anything else I can offer you, Mrs. . . . ?"

"Just call me Sadie. And yes, I would love one of your mint sticks."

The storekeeper lifted the top off one of the jars on the counter and handed her a pair of horehound sticks, saying, "I insist that these be a gift, Sadie."

"Why, thank you," she murmured, then added with a flirtatious lilt to her voice, "And perhaps I can repay your kindness someday soon, when my husband isn't feeling so poorly. The journey really did tire him out. In fact, I'm thinking of leaving him at home with the housekeeper and heading back this way alone.'' Her violet eyes flashed with anticipation, and for a moment her gruff voice almost sounded sensuous.

"If you make it back to Farmington, Sadie, don't forget to visit the Emporium."

She smiled, then opened her handbag and asked, "How much do I owe you for the whiskey?"

"Two dollars will cover it."

She rummaged around in her purse and finally held up a five-dollar gold piece. "I'm afraid I'll have to pay with my lucky gold coin—the one my father carried all during the Civil War. But there's no help for it. You see, for safety's sake we didn't bring much money to Santa Fe, intending to cash a bank draft. And then Arvis got sick and we had to leave. It was Saturday, so all the banks were closed, and we only had enough cash for the stage fare." She gave a long, lingering sigh. "Oh, well, there's no point being sentimental over an old coin."

"Why, Sadie, I wouldn't dream of allowing you to pay with such a keepsake. Especially not for two dollars' worth of whiskey. Forget the bill."

"But I insist on paying. If not with my lucky coin, then perhaps you would take a bank draft?"

"It's not necessary, but if you insist, then of course I'll accept it."

Grady pushed forward a pen and bottle of ink as Sadie unfolded a large piece of paper from her purse and spread it out on the counter. She began to fill out the draft, then paused and looked up at the elderly storekeeper. "I don't suppose . . . well . . . oh, never mind."

"What is it, Sadie?" he implored, again placing his hand over hers.

"I was just thinking about the long ride to Durango

and that I might have need for a little cash along the way. I was wondering if you would consider letting me make out the draft for something above the two dollars—say, for five dollars extra?''

Joseph Grady smiled as he patted her hand. ''Make it ten, Sadie. I insist.'' He reached down and lifted up a small metal box, which he placed on the counter. Then he opened the lid, withdrew a ten-dollar gold coin, and pressed it into Sadie's palm. ''I'll wait until you return to Farmington to collect my interest,'' he said with a telling wink.

As Grady closed the box and replaced it under the counter, Sadie glanced over at her husband. Arvis had made a complete circuit of the store, and now he was slowly making his way toward them, examining the goods on the shelves along the wall behind the counter. He looked up at his wife and smiled.

After helping his wife into the stagecoach, Stephen Davis climbed in and sat beside her. He quickly removed his hat and smiled at the attractive red-haired passenger seated on the opposite bench.

''Good day to you, ma'am. I'm Stephen Davis of Birmingham, and this is my wife, Merrilee. It looks like we'll be sharing the coach to Durango.''

''Pleased to meet you both,'' the woman replied, with a nod to each of the Davises. ''My name is Rebecca. Rebecca Williman.''

''Williman?'' Stephen asked, his pale eyebrows arching as he searched his memory. ''Haven't I heard that name before?'' He turned to his wife. ''You remember, Merrilee. It was the talk of Santa Fe. Something about a fire killing some millionaire mining investor.''

Merrilee leaned close to her husband and gently whispered, ''Perhaps she'd rather not talk—''

''No, that's all right,'' Rebecca interjected with a frosty smile. ''You're quite correct, Mr. Davis. The owner of the Williman Mining Company died last month when his house burned down. Hughes Williman was my father.''

"I'm so sorry," Merrilee sympathized.

"We were all sorry to lose him." Rebecca's hands clenched together, and she stiffened. Then she seemed to forcibly relax her body as she continued, "But life must go on—our own lives as well as the company's. That is why I am making this journey. As Hughes Williman's only child, the responsibility of running Williman Mining has fallen unexpectedly on my shoulders, and so I am on a tour to acquaint myself with the family mining interests." She paused, then asked, "And what brings you through New Mexico, Mrs. Davis?"

"Stephen and I are on our honeymoon," Merrilee replied, beaming a sudden smile. "We have been to New Orleans and most recently Santa Fe. Now we are headed for a ride on the new narrow-gauge railroad at Durango. Then we'll visit Pikes Peak, the hot springs at Manitou, and of course Denver. We'll finish with a steamboat cruise down the Mississippi."

Just then the door opened and Tom Kennedy looked into the coach, his gaze immediately locking with that of the arrogant young southerner. Merrilee lay a restraining hand on her husband's arm, but Stephen pulled free and leaned toward the door.

"Sir," he sarcastically addressed the black man, "certainly you don't intend riding *inside* this coach. You can see there are only two benches, with a lady present on each. I should think the driver has a suitable place for you up top."

Again Kennedy fought to control his anger. At forty-seven, he had long since given up trying to change the attitudes of others, and he had little desire to tangle with boys who thought they were men. But what really held him back was the look in the eyes of the southerner's wife.

He sensed something more than discomfort—perhaps a hint of compassion.

Seeing that an indignant Rebecca Williman was about to take the young southerner to task, Kennedy shot her a glance, as if to say that he preferred to handle the situation himself. He leaned back from the doorway and faced the wind, his hand shielding his eyes from the swirling dust. Then he turned back to Stephen, grinned, and said, "I think I'll take your kind advice. The air is so much cleaner out here." With that he nodded respectfully to Merrilee and Rebecca, closed the door, and walked away.

Stephen waited until he felt the coach tip under the weight of the black man climbing up to the roof seat. Then with a faint smirk he leaned toward Rebecca and boasted, "As long as I'm around, you won't have to worry about sharing your seat with a nigra. Not even out here in the *wild* West."

His low chuckle was cut short by the fierce glow in Rebecca Williman's eyes as she grabbed hold of his arm and firmly replied, "That *nigra*, as you call him, happens to be my friend, *Mr*. Davis. And you'd do well to call him by his given name. It's Tom Kennedy, and if you ever forget it, I'll be more than pleased to remind you."

From outside there now came a shrill flurry of oaths as the double doors of the nearby barn swung open and two stockmen emerged, each fighting a team of horses out into the storm and over to the waiting coach. The passengers pulled aside the leather window curtains and stared in awe as the four magnificent steeds stomped and snorted their way over to the wagon tongue, where they were quickly hitched to the traces. They stirred restlessly, more in anticipation of the journey than out of any fear of the wind.

Farther down the street, the door of the adobe stage office slammed shut, and a huge apparition came through the whirling dust. It looked like a huge bear, perhaps eight feet tall, but it walked with the grace of an athlete. And as it neared, the passengers could see that it indeed was the fur of a bear, but on the body of a lean, rugged-looking man in a flat-crowned hat. The tall man had added height; seated on his shoulders was a sandy-haired boy bundled in a thick wool coat—the same boy who had sat so silently on the bench inside the stage office.

As Quint Burgess reached the four-horse team, he leaned forward so that his son could pat each of the horses. Then Quint hoisted Lucas directly from his shoulders to the driver's box of the stage. He waved a greeting to the black man who was seated on the bench directly behind the driver's seat, then he walked around to check on the passengers inside the coach.

As he opened the door, Quint returned Rebecca's warm smile. Then he tipped his hat to Merrilee and Stephen Davis. "We're waiting on two final passengers," he explained. "We've already loaded their bags, and I'd hate to leave without them. We'll give them a couple more minutes, and then we roll."

Quint touched the brim of his hat, closed the door, and headed back to the front of the stage. He looked up and down the street for a moment, then put his thumb and forefinger to his mouth and cut the wind with a piercing whistle, first facing upstreet, then down. From out of the distance down the road, a large black object came bounding through the storm, and Quint immediately bent halfway over and grabbed hold of the spokes of the front wheel beside him.

As the black bullet raced closer, it took the form of a huge dog, and it made directly for the half-bent figure of Quint Burgess. Without slowing its pace, the dog leaped into the air, landed on Quint's back, then vaulted up to the high driver's seat overhead, where Lucas Burgess was waiting to throw his arms around him.

Quint stood up from the wheel, rubbed his lower

back, then climbed up to his seat atop the coach. He patted the dog's head and then his son's, accepting a sloppy kiss from one and a spirited hug from the other.

Inside Grady's Nickel Emporium, the elderly store owner stood back up after returning his cash box to its place below the counter. Sadie picked up the bank draft she had filled out and leaned forward to hand it to him, but in so doing, her elbow banged into her oversized handbag, which was resting precariously at the edge of the counter. Before she could grab it, the bag toppled to the floor at her feet, and its multitude of contents spilled all over. The two whiskey bottles, cushioned inside the bag, survived the fall and rolled out across the room, careening into the window mannequin and almost knocking it over.

"Oh, dear, my things," Sadie muttered, tears coming to her eyes as she backed away from the handbag. "I'm so sorry. It was so clumsy of me."

Joseph Grady hurried around the counter, stooped down on his hands and knees, and began to crawl across the room, stuffing the items back into her handbag. The trail led over to the mannequin—where Sadie now stood, Upon reaching it, he retrieved one of the bottles, then started looking for the other.

"I think it rolled over there," Sadie offered, pointing under a display case to one side.

Grady crawled over and groped around underneath, but found nothing.

"Try that bureau," Sadie suggested, pointing in another direction. But again a search revealed nothing. The same was true when Sadie directed him to look first under a stuffed chair and then under one of the green garden barrows.

"I think I see it, dear," Arvis called as he shuffled out from behind the counter and headed over to where Sadie was standing.

"Oh, you do, Arvis?" Sadie asked as Grady struggled back to his feet, puffing with exertion.

"Yes, dear, it's right under there." He pointed to a washstand hidden from view behind his wife's rather bulky form.

As Sadie moved away with an embarrassed smile, her husband reached down to retrieve the bottle. Instead, a half-dozen gold coins clattered to the floor, followed by a flutter of paper money.

Sadie's eyes opened wide with surprise, as did Joseph Grady's. The storekeeper stepped forward and stammered, "B-b-but I thought you said that five-dollar gold piece—"

"*Arvis!*" the woman suddenly shrieked. "Why, you no-good liar! You were holding out on me!" Then Sadie leaned over, grabbed hold of her husband's collar, and yanked him to his feet. "To think you made me leave Santa Fe without even buying a new dress! Said we couldn't afford it—didn't have any cash! And now this! How could you embarrass me this way? And after this kind storekeeper was good enough to cash our draft!"

What little color Arvis normally had was gone. He was shaking uncontrollably, and his wire-rim glasses were twisted on his face. Grady seemed even more embarrassed than his customers, and he immediately got back down on his hands and knees and began scooping up the coins and bills. All the while, Sadie kept raving at her husband.

"Were you planning to drink it all? Or was it for throwing away at the gaming tables? Do I give you so little spending money that you have to squirrel away your own and plead poverty when a woman wants to buy a new dress?" Suddenly she grabbed his ear and twisted it viciously. "You're less than worthless! You're *nothing*!" With that she smacked him soundly across the back of the head.

Grady stood up now, and he cautiously held out the money. Arvis tentatively reached a hand forward, but

Sadie roughly slapped it away. She picked up her open handbag and smiled coyly as Grady dropped the bills and coins inside.

"I don't know how to thank you," Sadie said, snapping shut the bag. "You've been so kind."

Speechless, the old storekeeper merely nodded and blushed.

Sadie pushed her husband ahead of her now, and he stumbled toward the door, which Grady quickly opened. Prodding her husband out onto the walkway, Sadie glanced back at the merchant and promised, "I'll return with that interest I owe you." Then she flashed a final smile and was gone, herding her husband before her.

Snatching up his overcoat and slipping it on, Grady stepped out onto the walkway, shut the door, and stood for a moment watching the couple depart. Then he scratched his head, shrugged, and picked up the ladder to return to fixing his sign.

As they made their way down the street amid the swirling dust and debris, Sadie Goode's voice was lower, though filled with the same bitter disdain. "Can't you do anything right, Arvis? Do you always have to be such a dolt?"

"But, dear," he meekly replied, "I did just what you wanted. While you kept him busy picking up your things, I emptied the cash box, didn't I?"

"And then dropped it right at the idiot's feet! How stupid can you be?"

"But we got the money, didn't we?"

"With little help from you! I'm warning you—if you mess up this stage heist, it's the last you'll see of me!" And with a loud "Harumph!" she struck Arvis in the back, nearly knocking the little man off his feet.

As Quint Burgess unwrapped the reins from the brake handle and laced them through the gloved fingers of his right hand, he looked up through the swirling dust, trying to make out the sky to the west. Though the wind had abated somewhat, the sky had grown noticeably darker as a thick sheet of gray clouds rolled overhead. A morning windstorm was nothing new on the New Mexico plains, but Quint was beginning to fear that today's whirlwind might usher in a cold October downpour—a storm that could have a far more serious effect in the Colorado high country ahead. With the safety of his passengers his first concern, he decided he had waited long enough, and so he released the brake and reached for the whip.

Just then Quint saw a middle-aged couple hurrying down the center of the road from the direction of Grady's Emporium. "Leaving for Durango!" he called as he lifted the whip in his free hand.

"Wait up, driver!" Sadie wailed, prodding her husband to a faster pace. "We're the Goodes! Don't go!"

"Come along. We're waiting," Quint called back, grinning as he watched them stumble over to the stage.

The door on the street side was thrown open by one of the inside passengers, and Sadie hiked her dress and pulled herself up into the coach, her husband giving her backside an ineffectual boost. Then she reached back down and yanked Arvis inside, pulling the door shut behind him.

Quint slapped the reins, and the horses leaped into their collars. All at once the stagecoach lurched forward, and in a moment it was gone, its rooster tail of dust indistinguishable from the windstorm through which it traveled.

Chapter Two

Mountain Laurel sat on an antelope hide that was spread before the small central fire of the adobe lodge. She stared into the glowing embers, her right hand absently tracing the intricate beadwork that adorned her buckskin blouse. Twice she glanced at the large cloth-wrapped bundle near the wall to her left, then quickly turned away. Her hand drifted up to her cheek to wipe away a tear, and she forced a smile.

Rising to her knees, the young woman leaned over and pulled the bundle close. She carefully untied the twine, folded open the cloth covering, and lifted the top item up in front of her.

It was a shirtwaist traveling dress, with a high collar, long sleeves that buttoned tight at the wrist, and a pleated front panel. The floor-length skirt, which had a four-inch-wide ruffled hem, was made of dark green velvet, while the bodice was fashioned of a lighter green muslin. Though Mountain Laurel was uncomfortable just imagining herself in the outfit, she could not deny that it looked far prettier and more colorful than the rough sketch her father had shown her in the Chicago mail-order catalogue.

After carefully folding the dress and placing it next to her, Mountain Laurel removed the second item from the package: a brown, knee-length, coarse wool cloak with fur-trimmed hood. She examined it a moment, deemed it warm and serviceable, and was pleased it would largely conceal the dress. She folded it in half and draped it over the dress.

From the ground beside her, Mountain Laurel lifted a silver hand mirror and gazed into it. Her smooth skin was a light nut-brown, though not as deeply toned as that of her fellow Ute tribeswomen. And while her high cheekbones and firm chin clearly carried the blood of her mother's ancestors, her delicate features and striking emerald eyes revealed the legacy of her father, Josiah Fox.

Mountain Laurel's long brown hair cascaded loosely around her shoulders, highlighted by a single thin braid at each temple. And though she was not yet twenty-two, her hair was already liberally streaked with gray—another gift from her father, whose prematurely gray hair had earned him the name Silver Fox when he first came to live with the Ute people thirty years ago at the age of thirty-five. Now his hair was pure white, his green eyes beginning to frost with cataracts, his breath painfully short, and his frequent coughs sometimes spotted with blood.

The young half-breed woman realized she should be changing into her new traveling outfit for the journey by stagecoach to Durango. Josiah Silver Fox would soon be coming for Laurel, as he called her, preferring to use the shortened Christian form of her name. In fact, Josiah had chosen the name Mountain Laurel because it bridged the two cultures. As a Quaker physician who had chosen to spend his life ministering to the Indians, he knew that although he was allowed to enter the world of the Indian, he would always be white. Likewise, in life Laurel's mother could share only a part of her husband's world. In death—which had come while giving birth to Laurel—she had returned to her Great Spirit, as Josiah would soon return to his Nazarene.

But Mountain Laurel Fox *was* the bridge. It was what

she had always been taught and had always believed. Yet now, as she prepared for her first journey from her mother's home to the land of her father, she did not feel at all American, but rather one of the People—a full-blooded Shoshoni Ute.

Laurel quickly rose and hurried from the lodge. She did not look toward her father's lodge, where a buckboard wagon was even now being hitched and loaded with thirty-five years of her father's memories. Instead she ran north toward the mountains, from which the eagles kept watch over the village and the People. She ran north to the Old One—to the cavern of Surnia.

The Old One sat cross-legged on the bare earth and slowly positioned another branch upon the fire. The flames danced and crackled as leaves caught and burst, and the flare of light cast flickering shadows across the cool, rough stone of the cavern walls. The thick billowing smoke spiraled upward and disappeared through unseen cracks in the high ceiling.

Surnia never glanced up as Laurel silently entered the chamber from behind him. He merely raised a hand and, crooking his finger, motioned her to sit opposite him.

As Laurel took her seat and stared across the flames at Surnia, she thought she detected a smile on his unyielding countenance—though she knew it was only the shadow of a smile, for the Old One never betrayed either his sorrow or his joy. At the same time, she could sense that his eyes held a glimmer of sadness at this leave-taking.

After several minutes of silence had passed, Surnia closed his eyes and said, "Today is the day that Mountain Laurel returns to the land of her father. It is a good day. But we have already said our farewells, this young flower and I. What brings her yet again to warm herself before my fire?"

"I do not wish to leave the village of my people. I

have come, Old One, so that you may tell me I do not have to go.''

Surnia's long, gnarled fingers snapped another section of branch and tossed it among the embers.

"It is not for me to keep the flowers from blooming," he replied. "The eaglet leaves its nest. The buffalo calf must in time forsake its mother's milk. And so, too, must the young Mountain Laurel find its own season and bear its own flowers."

"I have found my path here in the village, among the People. You have taught me the secrets of herbs and bark, the brewing of potions that can replenish and heal. From my father I have learned to set bones and to open and repair the body, closing it without harm. These gifts have been given me so that I may return them to our people. My father's people would have no use for gifts such as mine."

"But Mountain Laurel *will* go. . . .'' His whispered words were a blending of question and statement.

"Yes, Surnia, I will go if my father insists that it be so. This journey—this dream that I become educated at a medical school—is all that keeps him alive. He is a physician, and yet he cannot heal himself of that white plague—of the consumption." Her eyes turned downward, her shoulders sagging. "And in his pride he will not let you heal him."

The old man leaned forward and for the first time spoke directly to Laurel. "You are wrong, my child. It is not a white man's pride that separates Silver Fox and Surnia. I cannot heal your father because he does not believe I can heal. He believes only in the great power of his medicines, and his people have not yet found a pill to destroy this thing that eats him from within."

Laurel looked up with an eager light in her eyes. "But you could cure him, Surnia. I have seen you heal a cancerous lesion with herbs. You have even repaired a ruptured appendix without having to remove it with a knife.''

"Those are white man's fancy words," Surnia said, waving at the air and shaking his hand as if warding off an evil spirit. "That is your white tongue speaking. There is no place in my medicine for knowledge such as that. We do not divide the body into little pieces, breaking it apart and putting it back together like it was buffalo skin stretched over so many tipi poles. You have worked with me. You should know this. The body is a whole—every part connected and fed by the Great Spirit within. We apply herbs and potions like we lay buffalo robes over our elders in winter. It is not *they* that heal. They simply comfort us and allow the Great Spirit to heal from within.''

Laurel's voice softened as she asked, "May I speak to you of my father's medicine?''

Surnia laid aside the small pile of branches he was holding and folded his hands in his lap. He nodded, then fixed Laurel with a calm, unwavering stare.

"I have worked many years beside my father and have come to know the power of his medicine.''

As she spoke, Laurel turned away and looked down at the fire. She knew that thirty years earlier Surnia had struggled to keep Josiah Silver Fox from ministering to the Ute people. It was soon after Josiah's acceptance by the tribe that Surnia had left his lodge for good and had taken up residence in this cave, treating only those who sought his counsel. And when, out of an overpowering desire to learn more about the ancient ways of her mother's people, Laurel had sought out Surnia and convinced him to initiate her into the deeper mysteries of their faith, he had never mentioned her father. Indeed, until a few days earlier when Laurel had announced she was leaving, he had never once mentioned Josiah during the seven years he had secretly taught her the ways of a Ute medicine man.

"While it is true that he is unable to treat many

diseases," Laurel continued, "his chemicals and his knowledge of their uses have saved many Ute lives—lives that might have been lost in the years before he arrived among the People." As Laurel continued to speak, she found the strength to look up and face Surnia directly. "For seven summers I have been your student, and for seven winters I have been his. I have watched you cure many of our people he could not help. And I also have seen him succeed where you have failed. There is a middle path, and it is my dream to find it and make it mine."

For the first time since they had met, Laurel saw the Old One's face break into a broad grin. She watched in stunned silence as he stood, came around the fire, and lifted her to her feet.

"I have no more to teach you, my young Mountain Laurel. You have learned the greatest lesson of all—you have discovered who you are."

Surnia turned and led the way from the main chamber of the cave. When he reached the cavern entrance, he turned and stood silhouetted in a blaze of sunlight.

"You are right to honor your father's medicine. It holds great power—perhaps far greater power than I will ever know. I fought your father's coming not because I feared his medicine was stronger than mine. It was because I feared our people would turn from the ancient paths and would lose their connection to the Great Spirit that balances and gives life to all beings. In many ways, I was right. But I know now that there was no way to stop the coming of the white man—it was the will of the Great Spirit. And now I also know that our village was blessed that such a man as Josiah Silver Fox came first to prepare us for this strange future that will be ours."

Laurel approached and stood beside Surnia in the entranceway. Together they stared at the village in the valley below.

"But why, then, must I leave?" she asked. "Surely it is my path to continue the work of my father."

"We cannot know what the Great Spirit has chosen for each of us. But you are a Ute, and you must obey your father's wishes. Perhaps you will return with greater knowledge—with an even greater gift for our people."

"But already I am a physician. My father has taught me everything I would learn at one of those medical schools. It is only for a piece of paper that he takes me there. Even *he* admits it is his desire to see me receive that piece of paper—that diploma—that fires his dream. But the Ute have no need of paper. It is wrong for us to leave when our people need us most."

Surnia placed a gentle hand on Laurel's forearm. "My child, I do not pretend to know the thoughts of the Great Spirit. But isn't it possible that Silver Fox has another reason for this journey? A reason even he does not see?"

Unexpected tears welled up in Laurel's eyes. "You mean, because he is dying," she whispered.

"I do not know what is really guiding his footsteps, but perhaps Silver Fox must see his land once more and must share it with you before he can pass to the beyond."

They stood in silence, and then Laurel began to walk from the cave. After several steps, she stopped and turned to Surnia. "I will do as my father wishes, but in time I will return to my people. I will see you once again."

Surnia shook his head. "I will not be here when you return." Seeing Laurel's expression of shock and surprise, Surnia continued, "I am an old man—far older than your father. Before the Great Spirit calls me home, I must journey to the land of my ancestors. Soon the bluecoats will come and move our people west to their land of Utah, just as even now our Northern Ute brothers are being forced to make the terrible march. I will be gone before that day comes, and I will not return. I have no strength to see our sacred village destroyed and our people scattered to the wind.''

"But who will minister to the sick and injured? If the soldiers force us to leave our land, the journey to Utah will be long, and many will not survive. It is already being told how the Northern Ute are perishing on the long march west.''

"It is time for our people to choose their own way. Silver Fox will go in one direction, Surnia in another. It is now for the Southern Ute to decide. If they seek, they will find their answer—their future. Just as you will discover the path you must walk.''

"But how? Who will show me the way after you and Silver Fox are gone?''

Surnia raised his hand as if in greeting. It was the gesture he always used when they parted.

"Many teachers will come, if you have the eyes to see. It does not matter whether you are in the land of the Ute or of your father. But only by seeking within will the next teacher appear—perhaps taking the form of an eagle or teaching through the lips of a child. You may even discover his voice in the whispering of the wind.''

Mountain Laurel Fox raised her hand and returned the greeting of Surnia, the Old One. She gazed for a long moment at his wrinkled face, trying to capture the image of his sorrowful, compassionate eyes, his strong beak of a nose, his long, braided white hair, his eternally stern expression—trying to remember what he had looked like moments before when he had smiled. Then she turned and walked quickly away.

The Durango stage rolled north, the barren ground slowly rising toward the distant Colorado Rockies. The sky was an unyielding gray, thick and oppressive in its darkness. As the wind picked up outside, Stephen Davis leaned over and lowered the three leather curtains on his

side of the stage, tying them down to shut out the blowing
sand that had begun to billow through the windows. Beside him on the center of the rear bench, his wife, Merrilee,
leaned her head against his shoulder and affectionately
squeezed his arm.

Seated next to the window directly across from Stephen was Sadie Goode, who nodded her head at the young
southerner and graced him with an appreciative though
shallow smile. She turned and shot an impatient glance at
her husband, Arvis, who was trying to doze despite being
pressed awkwardly between her overabundant bulk on his
left and the far more appealing form of Rebecca Williman
on his right. When he failed to respond, other than to
yawn loudly, Sadie nudged him sharply with her elbow
and motioned with her head at the open windows beside
Rebecca.

"Shut them," she hissed under her breath.

Arvis came fully awake with a start, and for a moment he thought her command was in reference to his
eyes. Then he noticed the way she was nodding at the open
windows, and he realized someone had closed the curtains
on the opposite side.

Sucking in his breath and pulling himself free of her
oppressive bulk like a boot coming out of the mud, he
nervously leaned forward onto the empty center bench,
half crawled to the open windows, and reached up and
unfastened each one, rolling it down and tying it to the
bottom of the frame.

"Thank you," Rebecca said, removing her handkerchief from her mouth and taking a deep, relieved breath.
"That was most kind of you, Mr. . . ."

"Goode," Arvis informed her. He spun around on
the center bench and looked back at where he had been
sitting, noticing with dismay how his wife was already
expanding to fill the gap. Even as he debated trying to
squeeze back into place, Sadie began to fluff her dress and

wiggle left and right like a hen settling into place over its eggs.

Rebecca seemed aware of his predicament, and with her eyes she offered a sympathetic smile. Arvis sheepishly grinned at her as he sighed and settled back on the narrow center bench, accepting the fate of an awkward and uncomfortable ride on the backless seat.

"Mr. Goode," a gentle voice called from behind him. "Won't you join us on this side for a while? There is more than enough room."

Arvis turned around and faced Merrilee Davis. From the way the pretty and petite newlywed was nestled against her young husband, there indeed was plenty of room on the rear bench.

"Thank you very much," he replied as he slid back across the narrow aisle and took his place in the corner opposite Rebecca Williman.

Obviously annoyed by the attention her husband was receiving, Sadie summoned a fawning smile as she turned to each of the other women and declared, "Arvis *is* a dear, but he is so forgetful of the social amenities."

Patting some stray, imaginary strands of hair back into the severe bun atop her head, Sadie began to preen and puff herself up like a pouter pigeon. "I don't know what he would do without me. He was skin and bones when we met—not that he still couldn't stand a little more flesh on him. Why, you would think he never had a mother to teach him how to eat."

Both Rebecca and Merrilee looked noticeably uncomfortable during this soliloquy, but though they shared a few nervous glances, Sadie remained either unaware or unconcerned about their reactions.

With a deep, affected sigh, Sadie Goode plowed on. "Oh, well, I'm sure you women know what a trial men can be." She leaned forward to Merrilee Davis. "Of course, you are still such a young dear. You've so much yet to learn. But I'm sure that good-looking, considerate husband of yours will prove to be a cut above most.''

"Yes, Mrs. Goode,'' Merrilee agreed. "I am quite fortunate to have found a man like Stephen Davis.''

Stephen had been staring absently through the narrow gap along the edge of the window curtain beside him. He seemed to come alive under their praise, and he turned to his wife and shared a smile.

"What exactly is it you do, Mr. Davis?'' Sadie asked, fixing him with her most sincerely inquisitive expression.

"Do?'' he asked. "Why, our family has raised horses for several generations. Thoroughbreds, of course.''

"Of course. Where is your farm?''

Stephen smiled patronizingly and explained, "In Georgia, we don't refer to a thousand acres as a farm.''

Sadie's eyes sparkled with life. "Why, your family must own a plantation.''

"And soon Stephen will carry on the tradition,'' Merrilee interjected. Then, as if reciting a childhood verse, she added, "Cotton and cane for monetary gain. But nothing gives life like a horse and a wife.'' She giggled softly, and Stephen suppressed a blush.

Eyeing Merrilee's elegant fawn-colored dress, Sadie gushed, "That is such an attractive outfit, Mrs. Davis. And the way that gold trim highlights your lovely blond hair! May I be so bold as to ask if that is the current fashion in the East? It isn't easy to keep up on things out here in the wilderness. And of course, the cost of eastern fashions is so prohibitive.'' She casually fingered the material of her gaudy lime-green dress. "Why, even out here this old thing is at least two years out of style. Not that it is of any concern to Arvis.'' She shot a disdainful look at her oblivious husband, who was half asleep in the opposite corner.

Merrilee's smile was warm and genuine. "I think your dress is quite . . . appealing. And not at all out of fashion. As for my dress, it is just something we picked up on our way through New Orleans."

Sadie clapped her hands eagerly. "Why, then, it must be French! But I've heard they cost a king's ransom. How generous of your dear husband."

Stephen sat up straighter. Brushing away her comment with a mock air of indifference, he said, "It was nothing—barely a hundred dollars. Twice that much would be little enough to spend on my Merrilee."

Sadie swiveled in place and examined Rebecca Williman for a moment, sizing up the potential for profit. Rebecca's russet wool coat was open, revealing a black dress with a touch of gray lace at the throat. And unlike the lavishly adorned newlywed across the aisle, Rebecca wore no noticeable jewelry.

Adopting a motherly tone, Sadie offered, "If I may be so forward as to make an observation, you would look stunning in a dress such as Merrilee's." Glancing over at Merrilee, she added, "I *may* call you Merrilee, may I not? After all, I could be your mother." Without waiting for or even noticing Merrilee's affirmative nod, Sadie turned back to Rebecca and continued, "Now mind you, I have nothing against black, but your skin is so fair and lovely, and your red hair has such luster. You really should try something brighter and more gay."

Rebecca was not at all amused by Sadie's running commentary, but she tried to mask her displeasure.

Suddenly Sadie threw her hand to her mouth as if she had made an inexcusable gaffe. "Please pardon my presumption. Like mine, your financial condition may preclude such luxuries as the Davises are accustomed to."

Stephen leaned forward and said, "Don't apologize, ma'am. This here is Rebecca Williman. It's not due to any lack of monetary resources that she's outfitted so austerely. Rather, she's suffered the loss of a dear relative. Isn't that right, Miss Williman?"

Before Rebecca could respond, Sadie clasped her hands together and blurted out, "Why, you must be the daughter of that wealthy mining investor, Hughes Williman! Oh, how silly of me! From what I've heard, you could buy and sell each one of us several times over!"

Rebecca contained her growing anger and even tried to force a smile.

"It was all over the newspapers how your father's mansion burned down with him inside," Sadie barreled on, totally unconcerned about the effect her words might be having on Rebecca. "Oh, you poor dear! What a shock that must have been!"

Stephen could see how uncomfortable Rebecca was at Sadie's remarks, and feeling somewhat guilty about having first brought up the subject, he said, "Perhaps Miss Williman would rather not talk—"

"Of course she wouldn't," Sadie cut in. "It must have been so painful. Anyone could understand your wanting to take a little vacation to get your mind off things."

"Oh, no," Stephen interjected, as if coming to Rebecca's defense. "This is no vacation. It has fallen upon Miss Williman's shoulders to carry on the family business. That is why she and that—" he glanced at Rebecca before continuing "—that gentleman up above are making this journey. The Willimans have mines throughout Colorado, and it's now the reponsibility of this brave woman to make sure the Williman empire continues to prosper."

Sadie looked a bit taken aback. "You mean to say that you are traveling alone with that nigra up on the roof?"

With a firm gaze and a calm, controlled voice, Rebecca replied, "Mr. Kennedy was my father's most trusted employee—and as such he knows more about Williman Mining than any man alive. He was kind enough to accompany me on this tour of the mining region. He is both capable and trustworthy, and my family is lucky to have his services.''

Eyeing Sadie's shocked expression, Stephen Davis suppressed a smile and explained, ''That Mr. Kennedy is apparently one of the new breed of coloreds. He walks and talks—even thinks—like a white man. But who am I to disapprove? I haven't forgotten that we lost the war, and I suppose we'll just have to make the best we can with the new order of things. After all, this isn't Georgia. This is the West, and I suppose we have to expect things to be different in a land where heathen Indians drink whiskey with whites.''

Sadie adopted an innocent expression as she opened the large handbag at her feet and produced one of the bottles of whiskey from Grady's Emporium. ''You wouldn't think *me* a heathen if I offered you a little drink, now would you, Mr. Davis?''

Merrilee laid a restraining hand on her husband's arm. In a soft, yet nervous tone, she said, ''Thank you, ma'am, but my husband and I never drink.''

With an understanding nod, Sadie put away the bottle and leaned back against her seat. She fell into an unaccustomed silence. She had little need for further talk; she already had more than enough information.

Sadie was certain that the young fop sitting across from her would be an easy mark. Undoubtedly he carried a large, ostentatious wad of currency. And despite his wife's statement, it was clear from the light in his eyes when he saw the whiskey bottle that Stephen Davis was no stranger to strong drink.

His wife would be no problem at all. She was far too demure to offer any trouble, and snatching those tempting jewels off her bodice would be easier than plucking a chicken.

Rebecca Williman might prove to be a tricky one. She was no naive ingenue; in fact, she had the tough manner of a woman who had seen life and knew its vagaries. But it was nothing that a Colt .45 could not handle. And as the daughter of Hughes Williman, Rebecca certainly must be carrying a prize worth pursuing.

There was still the question of that Mr. Kennedy up top, and of course the stage driver. But Sadie knew she and her husband would have the benefit of surprise when the time came. It had always worked to their advantage in the past.

Sadie let her gaze finally settle on her husband's semirecumbent form. It was just like Arvis to sleep on the job, she thought. She only hoped he would be of some use when she decided it was time for them to act.

With a sigh, Sadie Goode leaned her head against the hard leather backrest and closed her eyes.

As the wind whistled across the open plain, Tom Kennedy leaned forward from his place on the bench behind the driver's seat and shouted, "You been driving this route a long time?"

Over his shoulder, Quint Burgess called back, "Ever since we opened the Farmington to Durango leg of the run last year."

Kennedy rested his hand on the shoulder of young Lucas, who was seated beside Quint with his big black dog wedged between them. "You ride with your pappy often, son?"

Lucas did not reply, though he did turn to look at the black man and made no effort to avoid his touch.

"It's not that he's unintelligent or impolite," Quint explained. "There's something wrong with his hearing, and the doctors say there's no cure. But he's not completely deaf. He can make out sounds, and he understands a lot of what people say. He just isn't much for talking."

"Yeah," Kennedy replied, breaking into a broad grin and patting Lucas on the back. "And don't you be ashamed of it, son. Not talking can get a man through many a scrape—something my people learned a long time ago."

"I'm glad you understand," Quint said. "There's a lot of folks who don't make the effort, Mr. Kennedy."

"The name's Tom."

"And I'm Quint." He reached across with his free left hand and grasped Kennedy's.

"The way I look at it," Kennedy continued, "you can better gauge a man's intelligence by the caliber of his actions than by what comes out of his mouth."

Lucas gave a fleeting smile, almost as if he understood their conversation. Then he threw his arms around the neck of his dog and hugged it affectionately.

Kennedy briskly rubbed the dog's fur. "That's quite an animal you've got there."

"We call him Little Bear—for obvious reasons," Quint explained.

"Nothing little about that bear," Kennedy joked, and as Lucas's grin broadened, he playfully tousled the lad's hair.

Suddenly Lucas leaned forward and peered through the swirling dust. He began to wave furiously into the distance.

"What is it?" Kennedy asked. "What's he see?"

"The ridge up ahead. You'll be able to make it out in a minute. It holds the first real gather of trees this side of Farmington, and it marks the beginning of the Southern Ute reservation. We should make the reservation way station within the hour. It's Lucas's favorite part of the trip."

"And I'm sure it will be mine," Kennedy agreed. He stared into the distance, then let out a playful whoop. "There it is, Lucas. I see it. Those trees sure look grand, and it's nice to see the ground with a little shape to it. I was getting awfully tired of those unending, flat plains. Why, son, I wouldn't be surprised if right now a couple of

Indian warriors were sitting among those rocks pointing down at us, just like we're pointing up at them!''

Indeed there were two men on the ridge, but they were not Ute warriors.

The shorter, better-dressed man pulled back on the reins to keep his horse steady. "Looks like the Durango stage is right on schedule, Custer."

"Why not hit it now?" his big, unkempt partner asked.

"That's stupid, when it's doing the work for us," the first man said. "We're all going north, so all we gotta do is let it get clear of Indian land and make our move this side of the Animas River. Anyway, I want a closer look to size things up."

"How we gonna do that, Ned?"

"Why, we'll just sit down and enjoy a good meal with those fine folks. Come on, Custer, we gotta ride if we're gonna make the way station ahead of that coach." He yanked on the reins, turning his horse, and led the way north at a gallop.

Chapter Three

As the faint, distant clamor reaching the ears of the stagecoach passengers grew louder and more distinct, it gradually became recognizable as a high-pitched, whooping and hollering chant. Each screeching cry pierced the interior of the coach like a flame-tipped arrow.

"*Indians!*" screamed Sadie Goode, her voice setting her husband trembling.

With numbed, shaking fingers, Arvis lifted the leather window curtain beside him and peered outside. He quickly let the curtain drop. As he turned back to the others, his face was blanched, his eyes as rigid as a corpse's. "*Indians,*" he repeated in a whisper.

At the other end of the rear seat, Stephen Davis was raising his curtain and tying it up. Merrilee leaned close beside him, and together they stared forward through the dust cloud raised by the horses' hooves. In the far corner of the forward seat, Rebecca Williman had already opened the window covering and was twisting around on the bench to get a better look.

Sadie began to sob softly as she muttered, "They'll kill us all. . . . They'll rape me, and then they'll torture us. . . ."

Arvis seemed to recover some color. His gaze drifted to his wife, and for a moment he appeared to be looking through her. Then suddenly he shook his head, as if coming out of a dream. He leaned forward onto the center bench and quite tenderly took Sadie's hands into his own.

"They won't touch you, my dear. I won't let them."

At his words, she ceased sobbing and merely stared incredulously at him. Then with a sudden yank, she pulled her hands away and threw them up to her face, burying a renewed flood of tears in her fleshy palms. Arvis remained as motionless as the rocking stage would allow, at a loss for how to comfort his wife.

"That must be the way station!" Merrilee called out.

"My God, they've massacred the stationmen," Arvis mumbled, his words punctuated by his wife's harsh wail.

"It's nothing like that," Rebecca said, turning to the Goodes. "That is the way station at the Ute reservation. I assure you, we are in no danger."

Sadie momentarily lifted her head from her hands and blurted, "That's easy for you to say! You're used to dealing with . . . with savages!"

"Nonsense!" Rebecca shot back, her patience wearing thin. "Don't be such a jellyfish. Look out the window!"

Shaken by the rebuke, Sadie did as commanded. Hesitantly she twisted around to face the window. She clutched the leather curtain, pulled it back slightly, and timidly peered with one eye through the crack.

The stage was rapidly bearing down on the way station, a long, single-story adobe structure with a dilapidated wooden barn behind it. Several dozen Indian women were clustered around the front yard, waving blankets and baskets as they joined in an eerie chorus of shrill, rolling wails, resembling more a chant for the dead than a call to market.

The crowd barely parted as the stage and team of four barreled through and pulled to a jarring halt in front of the station building. There was a split second of silence, then the throng leaped at the coach like starving wolves.

Sadie, still clutching the curtain, jumped as it was

yanked from her hand and pulled aside. A tiny, white-haired Indian woman, hanging precariously from the sill, thrust an emaciated arm through the window and shook an assortment of brightly colored beaded necklaces in Sadie's face. As the woman gained a toehold on the iron steps that hung below the door, she hoisted herself up, leaned through the frame, and gave Sadie a broad, toothless grin.

"Plenty good beads!" the woman insisted. "Real Indian beads! You like beads, pretty lady?"

Sadie, still sliding back from the window, shuddered and gave a low grunt of disgust. "Get away," she whispered, waving the woman off. *"Away!"*

The stage tipped to the left as someone climbed down from the box, and then the passengers heard Quint Burgess making his way to the door.

"Back now, women! Give us some room. There's plenty of time to sell your goods—just give us some room."

The old woman at the window gave a playful giggle as two strong arms reached up and pulled her back down from the stage.

"Pretty ladies like beads," she announced as Quint lowered her to the ground. "Pretty ladies buy my beads."

"Yes, Sings-With-Moon, I'm sure they will," Quint agreed. "And if they don't, you bring me a couple, and *I'll* buy them."

As Sings-With-Moon continued to giggle, Quint grabbed the doorknob and turned back to the crowd. "Now make some room," he called out. "There's plenty of time before we pull out for Durango."

The women settled down somewhat but held their ground. With a shrugging grin, Quint yanked open the coach door and looked in at the passengers. "We might as well get it over with. If you make it through this gauntlet, you'll be rewarded with a hot meal inside. Now, ladies first. And I suggest that you buy a little something, if at all possible. It's really the only way to get them to stop pestering you."

Rebecca Williman came forward first and accepted Quint's hand with a gracious nod. As she stepped down to the ground, Quint pointed her toward the building and released her to the mob. In a second she was lost amid a flurry of waving hands, shouting voices, and brightly embroidered deerskin dresses.

Merrilee was next, and she entered the fray with an eager, excited light in her eyes. Stephen held back a moment, politely waiting for Sadie Goode to make her exit. When it became clear that Sadie was nowhere near being ready to leave, he shrugged and quickly disembarked, hurrying forward through the crowd to catch up with his wife.

"Aren't you coming?" Quint asked the Goodes. "They won't hold the meal."

Arvis looked nervously at his wife, whose face was a mask of horror and disdain. Finally he turned to Quint and quietly said, "Don't worry about us. We'll be along in a moment."

Quint nodded and walked from the coach toward the horse barn. As he neared the corral, he glanced back and saw that Sings-With-Moon had again ventured up onto the iron steps and was boldly pushing her way into the stage, her beaded necklaces still outthrust in one hand. Even through the din of the crowd, he heard Sadie's cry of alarm, then caught a glimpse of her with carpetbag in hand, using it as a battering ram against the old Indian woman. He suppressed a chuckle as he continued on his way.

Tom Kennedy climbed down off the stage now. He looked back up at young Lucas Burgess and asked, "Are you coming?"

The boy quickly shook his head, then grinned and squeezed Little Bear's neck.

"See you later," Kennedy told him. Then he spun around and started for the building.

By now, Rebecca and the Davises had reached the

safety of the station house and were disappearing inside. As Kennedy crossed the yard, the swarm of Indian women spun around to eye their next potential customer. When they saw Kennedy, a sudden hush came over them. En masse, the women backed to the left and right, opening a clear pathway for the black man. Even Sings-With-Moon forgot her sale as she backed away from the stage and stared wide-eyed at the unusual stranger.

Noting what had happened, Arvis quickly turned to his wife. "Sadie, this is our chance. Let's go."

"But, Arvis—"

"We *must* go, dear. This is our only chance."

An involuntary shiver coursed through Sadie. Then she quickly clutched the carpetbag to her bosom, gave her husband a prod, and declared, "Let's get on with it, then."

Arvis fairly leaped from the stage. He offered his wife a hand, but she paid him no attention as she grasped the railing beside the door and lowered herself to the ground. Then the pair hurried behind Kennedy through the parted crowd.

From his perch atop the stagecoach, Lucas watched the Goodes hastening across the yard. His smile became a broad grin, then transformed into a chuckle, and finally a rolling laugh. In his mind, the woman had become an ugly, oversized duck, waddling awkwardly along the shore. Bobbing haphazardly behind was her nervous little duckling, his eyes darting left and right as he struggled not to get swamped in her wake.

As Lucas laughed, he hugged Little Bear tighter. The big black dog looked up, felt his master's merriment, and playfully began to bark.

Inside the main room of the way station, Merrilee showed Rebecca the small covered basket she had purchased, then admired the handwoven blanket Rebecca had been talked into buying.

"And what did you get, Mr. Davis?" Rebecca asked Stephen, who was jangling something in his hands.

"Oh, these? Arrowheads." As Stephen opened his palms and displayed the souvenirs, his voice became more animated. "The squaw said her son used them on Custer at the Battle of Little Big Horn."

"Weren't those the Sioux, not the Ute?" Merrilee asked innocently.

"Who cares," her husband replied, brushing the comment aside. "It was Indians." He took Merrilee by the arm and led her toward the table. "Come along, before everything is gone."

The Goodes had already taken seats on one side of the large, square table that dominated the room. Tom Kennedy was seated on the side to their left, and Rebecca headed around the table and took the place beside him. Across from the Goodes sat a pair of strangers who were already wolfing down their meal when the passengers arrived, so Stephen steered his wife to the remaining empty side, directing her to the chair nearest the Goodes.

As Stephen took his seat, he smiled at the men to his right and said, "Are you fellows joining our stage to Durango?"

The nearer man was smaller and better dressed, with a dusty brown suit and frayed string tie. He lowered the chicken leg from his mouth and, between swallows, answered, "Just passing through. Objections?"

"Of course not," Stephen replied, slightly flustered. "I was only trying . . ."

Just then a portly Indian woman entered the room bearing a fresh platter of chicken, which she placed before Stephen Davis. He had just pulled the dish closer and was lifting the serving fork when Tom Kennedy politely suggested, "Shouldn't we offer the ladies first?"

Stephen shot him an annoyed glance. "That's exactly

what I was about to do, *Mr.* Kennedy," he lied, holding the platter forward for Rebecca.

After Rebecca had served herself, Stephen held the platter first for Merrilee and then Sadie Goode. Finally he handed it to Arvis, who took a small piece of chicken and began to pass the dish to Kennedy.

"I'll take that next," Stephen declared, snatching the platter from his hands. Noticing that it held a large breast and two small legs, he took the breast, then deliberately added one of the legs to his plate. "I believe the rest is yours, Mr. Kennedy," he said with a grin as he handed over the dish.

His sport was short-lived, however, for a few seconds later the Indian cook reappeared with another platter piled high with chicken. Close on her heels came a burly, bearded man, who stood beside the table and waited until the woman had departed.

"Folks, my name's Halloran. I'm the stationmaster. Now make sure you eat hearty. It'll be a long night's ride, and this is the last meal before Durango." He started to turn away, then added, "Oh, yes, I'm afraid it'll be a bit more cramped from here on. Got yourselves a couple more passengers."

Stephen shot the two strangers a distrustful glance. As if reading his thoughts, the stationmaster continued, "It's not these two gents. They just stopped for a meal. The folks I'm talking about are a father and daughter. They're quite well known in these parts, and even you may have heard of them. Hear tell there's even a dime novel that makes the father into some kind of white prophet, with his daughter the beautiful half-breed heroine. But let me tell you, whatever is written, it can't do justice to either one of them."

"Do you mean Dr. Josiah Fox?" Rebecca asked.

"Exactly. Josiah and his daughter, Laurel. And it's a real honor to have them riding our stage. They're due here any moment, and you'll be pulling out right after."

As the man left the room, there was a rush of low murmuring among the passengers.

"Josiah Fox?" Sadie asked. "I don't know of any—"

"Surely you've heard of him," Stephen interjected. "He's even known in Georgia. Josiah Fox—the Silver Fox of the West."

Sadie almost dropped her fork. "You mean that fool Quaker who left civilization to live with a heathen squaw?"

"He went as a physician, Mrs. Goode," Rebecca corrected. "It must have been a good thirty years ago— well before the war. They say he fell in love with a princess of the tribe and married her. This Laurel must be their daughter."

"Well, whatever she is, it just isn't natural," Sadie insisted.

"But if they were in love . . ." Arvis tentatively offered before his wife's harsh gaze cut him off.

"If I say it isn't natural, Arvis, it isn't. Not at all what God had in mind when he sent us to civilize the West."

"My thoughts precisely, Mrs. Goode," Stephen agreed. "It upsets the ordained balance—muddies up the natural order and makes people lose sight of their place in the scheme of things." He gave Kennedy a knowing look.

Kennedy pushed his plate aside and leaned forward. "Mr. Davis, if you honestly believe God is pleased by what our country has done and continues to do to the Indians, we must be reading from different Bibles."

With a broad smile, Stephen replied, "That's quite likely, since mine is in English. Do you read English?"

"Tom reads both English and Spanish," Rebecca interjected, her stiff smile betraying her anger.

"Oh, *muy bien*," Stephen said with a twitter. "Isn't that the way it's said south of the border, Señor Kennedy? Well, in Georgia we believe good old American is all anyone needs to know."

Merrilee looked visibly uncomfortable. She leaned close to her husband and touched his forearm. "Stephen, dear, it's still a long way to Durango, and—"

"And it'll seem even longer with a half-breed on board," he interrupted. "By all rights, her place should be up top with the . . . with *Mr.* Kennedy."

"I know what you think of *me*, Mr. Davis," Kennedy shot back, "but even a man such as yourself—a refined and cultured gentleman of the South—would have to agree that, half Indian or not, this Laurel Fox is a woman. Surely you don't expect a woman to ride up top?"

"Well, I suppose we can't force her," Stephen relented, "but I just hope she was bred to keep quiet—unlike those heathen squaws outside." He turned to the others. "I don't care how well intentioned this Josiah Fox thought he was being, but living among the Indians and teaching them our ways only leads them to think they can be just like us—like real Americans. It's the same mistake those other Quakers in Pennsylvania made two hundred years ago. See where it's got us now?"

"According to the history books I've read," Rebecca said, "Pennsylvania was the only colony where the Indians and whites lived in harmony—thanks to a Quaker named William Penn."

"That's exactly the problem," Stephen continued. "He got the heathens thinking they were as good as white folks. Sure, things were fine for a hundred years or so, but he was just sweeping the problem under the rug for his great-grandchildren to have to clean up. If they had finished those savages off in the beginning instead of pushing them west and letting them get rifles and horses, we wouldn't be having such trouble out here today. Aren't I right?"

Stephen directed his final questions to the two strangers beside him. The bigger one was too busy gnawing on his fifth greasy chicken bone to be paying any attention.

His partner, however, seemed very much interested in all that was being said.

"Excuse me, friend," Stephen began, "but you look like you're from around these parts. What do you think of the Indian problem?" When the man did not respond, he continued, "Perhaps you know of these Ute savages. Has this Josiah Fox, with all his supposed good works, done anything but stir them up?"

The man took a quick gulp of water, then faced Stephen. "Stir up the Ute?" he replied. "Naw, they're nothing but a bunch of lambs."

"Well, dangerous ones, no doubt, if the behavior of those squaws outside is any indication. I'd say we may be in for trouble with these heathen lambs in the years to come."

The passengers grew quieter as the dinner progressed. A few minutes later, the front door opened and Quint Burgess entered. He removed his gray-felt plainsman's hat and nodded at the people around the table.

"Won't you join us, Mr. Burgess?" Rebecca asked with a smile.

"Thanks, Miss Williman, but my son likes to eat outside, so I'm going to have dinner with him on the back porch. Then I've got some work to do out back."

He disappeared into the back room, reappearing shortly with two plates piled high with food, which he carried outside. A few minutes later, he passed back through the main room on his way to the kitchen, his own plate already cleaned off.

A moment after he was gone, the front door was yanked open and one of the stockmen came rushing inside. "They're comin'!" He shouted. "Looks like the whole Ute nation!" As he quickly darted back outside, he slammed the door so violently that it sprang back open.

Sadie and Arvis were the first to the doorway, and the others had to peer around them to get a view. The afternoon light was rapidly waning, and the dark, billowing clouds gave the landscape an eerie gray cast. Yet despite the thin light, the passengers could clearly discern what appeared to be a shimmering ribbon of heat waves, like an undulating mirage that wound through the hills and wove its way toward the way station. As it topped the nearest rise, the mirage took identifiable form. It was clear now that the stockman had not exaggerated, for upwards of two hundred mounted and marching Indians were making a procession that was rapidly nearing the station. At the head was a buckboard wagon bearing a white-haired man in a gray overcoat and a woman in a brown, fur-trimmed cloak.

When the procession was still some distance away, it halted, and the white-haired man stood up on the wagon seat and turned to address the Indians. Even with his back to the station, his deep, commanding tone carried to the assembled passengers, who tried to make out his words but quickly realized it was in the Ute language. All they could discern was the closing sentence, which was in English: "May we meet again one day in the Great Spirit that is love."

From nearby, an aged Indian in an elaborate feathered headdress kneed his mount closer to the wagon. The old warrior—apparently the chief—solemnly removed the headdress and held it out to the white man on the buckboard. There was a moment's hesitation, and then the man reached forward and accepted the gift. He stood watching as the chief turned his horse and slowly started back the way he had come. The rest of the column continued forward, filing past the wagon and then turning and following after the chief.

The passengers watched spellbound for a full fifteen minutes until the entire column of marchers had passed the wagon and had turned back into the hills. The rear of the procession was taken up by the Indian women who had accosted the stagecoach, their customers now all but forgotten. When all were gone, the white man sat back down, slapped the reins, and continued to the way station. As the wagon approached, the passengers noticed the striking similarities in appearance between the man and the young woman seated beside him. It was obvious that this was Josiah Fox and his daughter, Laurel.

The elderly man turned the buckboard in a wide circle and halted it beside the coach. A young brave appeared in the back of the wagon now, and he stood up and tossed the traveling bags to the ground. As soon as the wagon was empty and Josiah and Laurel had stepped down from their seat, the brave climbed to the front, picked up the reins, and started after the distant column of Indians.

"White heathens," Sadie murmured under her breath as she turned and barreled through the other passengers on her way back to the dinner table.

Laurel Fox stood nervously beside the stagecoach as her father supervised the loading of her bags by the hostler. Her attention was on the small knot of people crowded in the doorway of the station house. She wondered if she looked as awkward in her cloak and green velvet dress as she felt.

Suddenly Laurel was conscious of the fact that she was not wearing a hat. All white women wore hats, or so the pictures in the catalogues seemed to indicate. But worse than that, Laurel had left her hair hanging loose upon her shoulders, the only adornment being the two beaded braids at the front of each side. Even a naive half-breed from the reservation knew that proper women— proper white women—wore their hair up, reserving such styles as Laurel's for the boudoir.

A gentle hand touched Laurel's shoulder, and she spun around to see her father smiling at her.

"Laurel, dear, why not wait here while I go inside and pay for the tickets?"

"Why, yes, Father."

She watched him walk toward the station house and saw how the crowd in the doorway melted away as he approached. Soon after he disappeared inside, the other passengers began to drift out onto the porch and then into the yard. They seemed reluctant to near the stage, however.

Laurel noticed then that a small boy was seated off to one side on the porch, alone except for the large black dog beside him. The child had an eager light in his eyes as he stared at the distant hills, into which the Ute column had receded. The dog's attention was focused on Laurel, and his great tail was vigorously whisking the porch planks.

Forgetting the passengers, Laurel kneeled down and held forward her open palm. She gave a short, shrill whistle, following it with a gentle but firm "Here, boy!"

The large dog hesitantly stood to his feet. He seemed eager to approach, but he kept glancing back at his young master for approval. The boy did not seem to have heard Laurel's whistle, and his eyes remained locked on the horizon. The dog turned to Laurel, then looked back at the boy. Receiving neither permission nor denial, the dog ventured a few steps toward the edge of the porch. Again he checked the boy but received no answer. Finally making up his mind, the dog leaped gracefully from the porch and bounded over to Laurel, who playfully began to rub his thick fur. In return, the animal affectionately nuzzled her neck.

Ned Purvis and Custer Vance remained inside the station house, seemingly uninterested in the arrival of the Indian procession and the noted Quaker physician. Finishing his meal, the shorter man painstakingly brushed off his brown suit jacket, stood up from the table, and motioned for his burly companion to follow.

"Let's go, Custer," he said, leading the way to the open front door.

Vance quickly swallowed a huge mouthful of pie.

"Sure thing, Ned," he muttered as he stood and followed his partner, his beefy hands haphazardly tucking in the front of his flannel shirt, which only barely covered his bulging potbelly.

As they stepped out onto the porch, Purvis glanced around. Eyeing young Lucas seated cross-legged off by himself, his dinner tray on his lap, he called out, "Hey, kid, run out back and fetch our horses. And make sure they've been well watered and grained."

As if hearing a distant sound but not knowing from where it had come, Lucas put down his fork and stared out at the hills beyond.

Purvis turned to step off the porch, then noticed that the child had not responded. "Boy, get a move on. It's getting late. Fetch our horses."

When again there was no response, Purvis stomped across the porch, his boots rattling the boards and raising small dust clouds. He stopped directly in front of Lucas, purposely blocking his view.

"Now, boy, I told you to get our horses, so get up off your butt and see to it."

This time Lucas raised his head slightly and stared quizzically at Purvis.

"Dammit, boy . . ."

When Lucas's expression remained unchanged, Purvis leaned down, grabbed hold of his collar, and with a cruel twist, yanked him to his feet. As the dinner tray crashed to the floorboards, Lucas emitted a high, piercing howl, his body wriggling wildly in an effort to free himself.

From across the yard, Laurel looked up and saw Ned Purvis grabbing and shaking the frightened boy. At the same instant, Little Bear saw it as well, and he immediately dashed across the yard, took one leap onto the porch, and a second at the stranger who was attacking his master. Like a steel trap, his jaw snapped shut around the man's wrist, forcing him to release Lucas.

With a screaming oath, Purvis spun around and began to strike Little Bear, trying desperately to free his other hand. "Custer! Dammit, help me!" he shouted at his partner, who momentarily seemed at a loss for what to do. Then Vance drew his Colt revolver and leveled it at the dog.

Laurel was already hurrying forward when Vance raised his gun. Just as the big man drew a bead on the animal and was squeezing the trigger, she raced up onto the porch and knocked his arm upward, making the shot go wild. Vance retaliated by slamming the gun back down, striking Laurel on the shoulder and upsetting her balance. But she managed to grab hold of his gun arm and hang on. Disregarding his partner's predicament for the moment, Vance wrapped his free hand around Laurel's waist, lifted her off her feet, and began to give her a bone-crushing, one-arm bear hug.

The scuffle drew the other passengers over, but they seemed either unwilling or unable to help. The gunshot alerted Quint, as well, and he now came dashing out of the station house. Seeing that Little Bear was capably taking care of the smaller man, he turned his attention to the man's partner, who was several inches taller than Quint and at least fifty pounds heavier. Snaking an arm around the big man's neck, Quint grasped his other wrist and yanked back, cutting off the man's air.

As Vance gagged helplessly, his hands went numb and his gun clattered to the porch. He lost hold of Laurel, and she fell stunned to the porch. Vance squirmed in agony for a moment as he shook his head to clear the fog that was rapidly filling his brain. Then he reached up with both hands and grabbed hold of Quint's forearm, locking it in a viselike grip and pulling forward to relieve the pressure on his neck.

Quint knew he would have only a moment to act before the big man managed to catch his breath. Vance was already beginning to lean forward and would soon lift Quint right off his feet and flip him off the porch. To forestall this, Quint moved deftly to the side and slid one of his legs in front of the man. Vance was still trying to pull the arm from his neck, when Quint suddenly relaxed his muscles, let go of his wrist, and released the choke hold. The resistance gone, Vance found himself yanking on nothing, and with some help from a shove by Quint's other hand, he lost his balance and went toppling forward off the porch.

Vance rolled once and was up like a cat—a huge, furious cat. Before Quint had any chance to react, the man came charging back up at him, catching him full force in the stomach. Quint was thrown backward off his feet, and he slammed against the wall of the building and slumped groggily to the floor.

As Quint shook his head clear, Vance savagely advanced for the kill. But a thunderous boom stopped him in his tracks. The big man spun around and found himself facing his own revolver, which was smoking in Laurel's hand.

"Lady, I wasn't doin' nothin'," he insisted as he backed away from her. "Just tryin' to help my friend."

Across the porch, Ned Purvis was still struggling to shake himself free of Little Bear, who was fastened on his arm with no intention of letting go. "Get this damn dog—" Purvis shouted between painful grunts.

"Little Bear, release!" Quint shouted as he got to his feet. On command, the animal let go of Purvis's arm and backed off slightly, ready to spring into action again if needed.

Laurel handed Quint the revolver, and he wagged it at the two men, ordering them off the porch.

"We done nothin', mister," Vance insisted.

"Yeah," Purvis agreed, rubbing his arm. "All I did was ask that idiot boy to fetch our horses, and next thing I know, that vicious beast was attacking me."

"Maybe it was the way you asked," Quint replied.

"That dog oughta be shot," Purvis continued, "the way he was tearing the hell out of my arm."

"I don't see any blood," Quint said. "But there will be, if you two don't get on your horses and ride." He motioned them toward the horse barn.

"What about my friend's gun?" Purvis asked. "This is Indian country." He looked disdainfully at Laurel.

Quint noticed that several of the stockmen were on hand now, each bearing a handgun or rifle. Raising the barrel of Vance's revolver, he opened the chamber and spun the cylinder until all six cartridges had spattered to the dust. Then he tossed the Colt toward the corral. "Now, mount up and ride."

Vance stood his ground and glared at Quint, as if ready to pounce again, but Purvis pulled at his companion's shoulder and led him away.

As the two men rode out of the yard, Custer Vance reloaded the revolver he had retrieved from where Quint had tossed it in the dust. With a last bitter look at the way station before it disappeared behind a hill, Vance asked, "We gonna let them run us off like that?"

"Wait your time," Purvis replied. "That stage'll soon be ripe to be plucked, and our revenge will taste all the sweeter."

"If it wasn't for that damn squaw . . ." Vance muttered sullenly.

"Don't worry none about her. I've got more than a few ideas what to do with that pretty half-breed vixen," Purvis promised. "Before we kill her."

Chapter Four

"**T**he stationmaster tells me your name is Quint Burgess."

Quint turned to see Dr. Josiah Fox standing in the doorway behind him. "Yes, Dr. Fox. Pleased to meet you."

"The name's Josiah." Shifting his gray overcoat from his right arm to his left, he held out his hand and smiled. "I was inside purchasing my ticket when that . . . that unfortunate scuffle took place." He coughed lightly, then continued, "I saw what you did from the window, Quint, and I sincerely want to thank you for helping my daughter the way you did."

When Quint shook Josiah's hand, he was surprised at the strength of the elderly man's grip. Equally impressive was the man's singular appearance. Snow-white hair and a trim beard framed his tanned, rugged features, and he was almost as tall as Quint, with the green eyes and supple build of a cat. His three-piece gray suit and gold pocket watch gave an added touch of distinction.

"It's really your daughter who deserves the credit," Quint insisted, "the way she stepped right in and helped my boy." Quint turned around to thank Laurel, but she had moved away across the porch and was standing near Lucas, who was energetically hugging his dog.

"You've probably been told that we purchased tickets

to Durango," Josiah said, regaining Quint's attention. "If you have no objections, we'd be honored to ride on your coach."

Quint's lips curled into a half grin. "Object? Well, Dr. Fox—Josiah—I've transported patent-medicine imposters, drunken whiskey drummers, crooks, card sharks, and painted women of, shall we say, dubious virtue. And not once did any of them seek my approval—not with a ticket in hand. But as for you and your daughter, not only do I not object, I am pleased to be the man at the reins."

"Good." Josiah's own grin broadened. "Then we won't keep you waiting any longer." He looked across the porch and called, "Laurel, it's time we boarded."

As Laurel turned to the two men, the brisk evening wind caught her hair and blew it across her cheek. She raised her hand and swept it back over her shoulder. The thin light of dusk accented the gray streaks that highlighted her hair, and at that moment Quint was struck by how young she appeared despite the premature gray—how it actually enhanced her striking looks. He especially liked the way she let her hair hang loose and long. It seemed to embody both her tall, statuesque beauty and her air of uncompromising independence.

Laurel approached and held out her hand to Quint. "Thank you so much for helping me," she said with a warm smile.

Quint shook her hand, then nervously let go and stammered, "Oh, it—it was nothing." He quickly turned to the other passengers and announced, "Time to get boarded."

As Laurel and Josiah stepped down off the porch into the dusty yard, Quint called to his son, "Come on, Lucas, let's be off."

Lucas immediately looked up at his father, then glanced toward the stagecoach. Noticing that Laurel was walking away across the yard, his jaw tensed and his eyes darted left and right, as if he were seeking something. Suddenly he lunged at the forgotten food tray, snatched up something, and clutched it tightly to his chest.

Lucas bounded off the porch and raced across the yard, Little Bear in lively pursuit. When he came up behind Laurel, he reached out with one hand as if to tug the back of her cloak. But just before touching the material, his hand pulled back nervously. Instead, he raced around the tall woman and planted himself in her path, a tentative grin on his face.

Laurel's eyes opened questioningly as she smiled back at him. Hesitantly, Lucas pulled his hands from his chest and held forth a large, ripe apple.

"Why, thank you," Laurel whispered, accepting the gift. As her fingers closed around the apple, the boy quickly pulled back, as if he was afraid their hands would touch. She was about to ask his name, but he was gone as quickly as he had appeared. She spun around to see him race up beside the stage driver, who wrapped a protective arm around his shoulder. Noting their facial features, she realized at once that they were father and son and that one day the boy would be as tall and good looking as his father. *And as strong and compassionate, as well*, she thought.

"Miss Fox," Quint began as he came up beside Laurel, "I'm Quint Burgess, the stage driver. There was something I meant to say back on the porch. . . ."

"Yes?" she asked as his voice trailed off.

"I . . . I want to thank you for helping my boy, Lucas."

Laurel looked over at the boy, who hung back behind his father. Then she smiled at Quint. "He is shy."

"It's just his way . . . ever since his mother died." Quint wondered why it was suddenly important that this stranger know his wife was no longer alive, and as he chided himself for his insensitivity, his smile hardened and faded.

"I am sorry about your wife," Laurel softly replied, misreading his expression as stemming from the pain of a recent loss—a loss that in reality had occurred more than four years earlier after almost six years of ill health.

The other passengers were approaching the stage-coach now, but they held back, as if waiting for someone else to make the first move.

"May I help you into the coach?" Quint asked Laurel as he opened the door.

"Thank you, but I'll wait for my father."

Quint nodded, left the door open, and headed forward to check the animals.

Laurel stood facing the Goodes and Davises, trying to smile but feeling more than uncomfortable under their combined gaze. Then she saw her father approaching and turned to greet him. He was walking with a friendly looking black man in a leather jacket and derby hat, and they were chuckling over some private joke. Laurel winced when Josiah's laugh disintegrated into a string of rasping coughs.

"L-Laurel," Josiah gasped as his coughing subsided. His grin returned. "I would like you to meet Mr. Thomas Kennedy. Tom, this is my daughter, Laurel."

"Pleased to meet you," Kennedy said, taking her offered hand.

Laurel smiled at Kennedy and replied, "The pleasure is mine."

"Won't you join us in the coach, Tom?" Josiah asked, but Kennedy shook his head ruefully.

"Sorry, sir, but I have a fine seat up top with the driver."

"Which is also the proper place for a half-breed to ride," Stephen muttered to Sadie with a snicker. His unsolicited comment was spoken just loud enough to be heard. As Laurel flashed him a look of anger, he continued, "Did you see the way she took on that big fellow back there? Fisticuffs on the porch, can you imagine that? And those heathens are supposed to be civilized."

Sadie snorted loudly in agreement.

Quint, who had just finished helping Lucas and Little Bear up onto the driver's seat, came up behind Stephen Davis now, and he looked far from amused.

"Perhaps if you had been man enough to step in," Quint remarked pointedly, "Miss Fox would not have been forced to engage in 'fisticuffs,' as you put it. I call it bravely coming to the aid of a young boy."

Stephen spun around, looking somewhat embarrassed. "It would've been crazy to go up against a gun. And it's not like he was going to use it on the boy—just a dog."

Quint stiffened, and he looked ready to strike the young man. But he took a deep breath and relaxed his hands. Turning to Merrilee Davis, he politely said, "I think you had better get your husband inside the stage, ma'am."

Merrilee nervously tugged at her husband's arm, and he reluctantly approached the open door of the stage. He helped his wife inside, then began to step up himself. At the last moment, however, he turned to Laurel, gave a sweeping flourish of his arm, and said, "Ladies first, of course."

Laurel brushed past Stephen and walked over to Quint. In perfect, unaccented English, she said, "Mr. Burgess, I had hoped you would permit me to ride up above." She glanced pointedly at Stephen Davis. "I do not wish to be the cause of any dissension among the passengers, and I can fully understand their concerns. After all, isn't it a known fact that Indians commit most of their savagery in the dark? And don't we prize a blond scalp above all others?"

Quint suppressed a smile. "You are most right, Miss

Fox, but there really is no need to put yourself out like that. Mr. Davis did not mean his comments seriously. He is really quite a man of culture—raised in a genteel land where, until recently, you could buy not only a scalp, but the entire man.''

With a stinging glare, Stephen Davis vaulted into the coach and pulled the door shut behind him.

"You handled him very well," Quint complimented Laurel. "I don't think you'll be bothered anymore."

"But really, Mr. Burgess—"

"Quint."

"Really, Quint, I would prefer sitting up top with you and your son. This may be the last time I see my home for a long while, and I would like to do that in the open."

"If that is truly your preference, Miss Fox, then yes, I would be delighted if you would join us above."

"Thank you, but only if you will call me Laurel."

"Agreed."

By now, the Goodes had joined Stephen and Merrilee in the coach, with Rebecca Williman having already boarded on the other side. Laurel approached her father and walked with him to the door.

"Would you mind if I rode above?" she asked.

"Of course not, Laurel." He leaned over and gave her a gentle kiss, which was interrupted by a short coughing spell.

With a look of concern, Laurel said, "Perhaps I should ride inside, after all. Your cough is getting worse."

"Nonsense," Josiah replied. "It's just the wet weather. You go ahead and enjoy yourself up top. Doctor's orders."

"Are you sure you will be all right?"

"Certainly." Josiah looked around, saw Stephen Davis and Sadie Goode staring out the windows nearest him, then noticed Tom Kennedy standing by himself near the front of the stage. "On the other hand," he added thoughtfully, "I would feel much more secure if that kind

Mr. Kennedy would agree to forsake his fine seat on top and would join me inside.''

Sadie and Stephen looked fit to burst. Quint quickly stepped forward, pulled open the coach door, and said, "I think that's a wonderful idea. How about it, Tom?"

As Kennedy hesitated, Josiah held forward his arm and asked, "Would you be so kind as to assist me into the coach?"

Kennedy glanced briefly at the passengers on board, found himself grinning, and took hold of the elderly man's arm. "I'd be delighted, Josiah," he said, and in a moment the two men were inside the coach.

Quint shut the door behind them and walked over to where Laurel was waiting. As she took his offered hand, they stood for a moment, sharing a warm smile. Then she broke the tension by asking, "Pardon me, but isn't this the stage to Durango?"

"I suppose it's time we found out," he replied, and she laughed softly as he gently boosted her to the seat high above.

The night had turned sharply colder, and the leather windowshades were lowered and tied in place. The oil lamps outside at the sides of the driver's box cast ruddy sunbursts upon the forward shades, filling the interior of the coach with a faint, flickering light.

The faces of the passengers on the rear seat—Stephen and Merrilee Davis, with Josiah Fox to their left—glowed pale, almost unearthly, softening and blending their features. On the forward seat, Sadie Goode sat across from Stephen, with her husband in the middle and Rebecca Williman to his right. One side of each woman's face was brightly illuminated by the lamplight at each window. Between them, Arvis was imprisoned in blackness.

Alone on the center bench, Tom Kennedy leaned back against the door between Rebecca and Josiah and savored the shadows of the night.

The silence was tangible and somewhat uncomfortable—broken only by the rumble of the stage and an occasional sharp inbreath from Stephen, who had fallen asleep on his wife's shoulder. From the way Sadie periodically nudged her husband beside her, the other passengers assumed Arvis also was on the verge of sleep, and they were surprised when his thin, reedy voice addressed Josiah Fox.

"Doc, I hear tell you spent thirty years living like an Indian. Is that true?"

Josiah chuckled lightly. "Yes, it is true that I have lived with the Ute—even *like* a Ute, I suppose. Exactly thirty years, in fact. It was the summer of 1851, two years after graduating Geneva Medical College in upstate New York, when I came out here."

"How could you stand it, all that time?" Arvis asked, his question born of genuine curiosity, with no hint of sarcasm or disrespect.

"The Ute manage to stand it a whole lifetime," Josiah patiently pointed out. "They even thrive. At least when we civilized folk let them."

"Well, more's the credit to you," Arvis replied. "My wife and I wouldn't last thirty minutes, let alone thirty years."

"Are you from these parts, Mr. Goode?"

"Out here? No. Chicago."

Sadie quickly twisted around to face them. "Why, Arvis, dear, you're such a caution," she interjected, then turned to Josiah. "We honeymooned in Chicago, and now you'd think that was all he could talk about. Actually, we've had our share of homes, but the last three years we've been settled in Durango."

"Really?" Josiah asked, his eyebrows arching. Across the aisle, Tom Kennedy leaned away from the wall and stared curiously at Sadie.

"Oh, it's a lovely town," Sadie continued, oblivious to the looks the two men were giving her. "But the only place to shop is Santa Fe, which is where we've just come from."

"That sure is something," Kennedy commented.

"Well, I wouldn't expect a man of your station to know where the best fashions can be bought," Sadie replied disdainfully as she turned from the black man.

"I wasn't referring to Santa Fe," Kennedy explained, baring a mischievous grin. "But you and your husband must be quite the pioneers to have spent three years in Durango, seeing as how it only sprang up a year ago, when the railroad arrived. Before that it was Ute land, which must explain why you got on so well with those squaws back at the way station."

It was only thanks to the orange lamplight that no one saw how bright Sadie's face flushed. "Did I say Durango?" she quickly recovered. "Of course it's only a year old. When I said three years, I meant Colorado."

"I see," Kennedy replied with less than full conviction as he leaned back against the wall.

"And as for my concern about those squaws," she continued, "if Custer had been half as cautious at Little Big Horn, he might still be alive to buy his wife a few of their trinkets." Her expression was smug and self-satisfied.

Josiah Fox looked thoughtfully at Sadie. "Unfortunately, those trinkets may spell the end for what once was a noble, even enviable, way of life."

"Trinkets?" Sadie asked incredulously. "But how could trinkets . . . ?"

"Not the trinkets in and of themselves, Mrs. Goode, but what they stand for," Josiah explained. "In the old days, the Ute were completely self-reliant, hunting and farming to feed themselves and their families. But as the demand for their artworks and artifacts has increased, the Ute have grown accustomed to relying on what they can sell to the white tourists in order to buy their food and other supplies. This, in turn, has led them to become lazy."

"The only good Indian is a lazy Indian," Arvis jested, but his tittering laugh ended in an abrupt grunt as his wife's elbow jabbed him in the side.

"Being lazy's something Arvis knows all about," Sadie lamented.

Asleep across the aisle, Stephen Davis was doing his own private lamenting. As he dreamed, the stage jostled him back to the daily horse rides of his youth, his best friend Willie invariably struggling to keep up on the back of some older, less enthusiastic animal.

A montage of mornings blended into one nine years ago, in 1872—a secret bareback ride at dawn aboard the one horse he had been ordered never to take out on his own. With only a mane to hang on to, his skinny legs clutching the big thoroughbred's sides, Stephen felt the thrill of the wind and the illicit excitement of his flight atop Cyclone, from whose loins the future generations of Davis thoroughbreds were to come.

At twelve, Stephen was already an accomplished horseman. Even Willie's pappy said so, and his pappy had been top groom at the Davis plantation for thirty years, ever since Stephen's father, Frederick Davis, had won him on a bet at a horse race. But that was before the Civil War, when Willie's pappy was a slave and Stephen's father was Massa Frederick. By 1872, that world had changed forever. Though at the end of the war Frederick had skillfully managed to retain his plantation, the slaves now were paid laborers, with Frederick Davis their employer. One day that job would fall to Stephen, and no one doubted that he would run the plantation as successfully as Frederick—just as Stephen never doubted that Willie would follow in his pappy's footsteps as chief groom and trainer.

The ride that morning had been doubly clandestine, because recently Frederick had announced that Stephen was too old to be associating any longer with the servants—

Willie included. To smooth the transition, Willie was ordered to work in the fields. "Best way to put muscle on the lad," his father had explained.

Yet Willie had agreed to go riding with Stephen that dawn, fearful of breaking Frederick's edict but just as unwilling to countermand an order by his son. Stephen had made quite a joke of it when he had demanded, "Hey, nigger boy, fetch Bethany and Cyclone and come for a ride with your Massa Stephen." It seemed such sport to Stephen, and Willie hesitantly had taken up his laughter, masking the bitter pain that suddenly filled him—a pain that had entered never again to leave.

But now in his dream, Stephen saw the wall his laughter had created, as tangible as the most intricate of spider webs. And as he looked upon his friend's dark eyes, for the first time he recognized the pain.

Stephen watched Willie and himself race bareback across the newly plowed fields, Cyclone four lengths in the lead, Bethany snorting and slipping farther behind. Stephen raised his head into the wind and cried with delight. Beneath him, the thundering hooves of his mythic steed traversed the soft loam as smoothly as a clipper crossing the ocean.

Suddenly there was a wrenching shudder and a splintering snap, and Stephen was flailing and flying as everything rushed into blackness. As the darkness slowly cleared, Stephen could see his horse lying dead in the mud. He felt himself pointing his finger at Willie and screaming, "Willie did it! Willie was riding him! Willie did it!" Then all that remained was the hurt look of betrayal in Willie's eyes . . . those dark eyes of pain, those accusing eyes, those eyes that kept calling him back.

"Stephen . . . Stephen, wake up," Merrilee called in a soft but urgent voice as she shook her husband awake.

He bolted upright, his eyes wide, a trailing scream still quivering his lips.

Tom Kennedy leaned forward, ready to steady Stephen, who looked in danger of toppling from his seat. "It's all right," Kennedy said as he took hold of the young man's forearm. "It'll be all right."

Stephen's eyes focused on his surroundings, the faint light of the oil lamps casting an eerie glow through the interior of the stagecoach. Finally his gaze rested on the dark eyes of the black man in front of him, and the word "Willie," soft and anguished, escaped from his lips. Then he seemed to remember where he was, and he quickly yanked his arm away from Kennedy, who shrugged his shoulders and backed away.

"What happened?" Stephen asked his wife.

"You were sleeping and must have had a nightmare."

"I—I'm sorry if I disturbed you," he apologized, looking at the other passengers—including Kennedy—each of whom insisted it was nothing to feel bad about.

Rebecca Williman could see that the young southerner was still quite shaken and embarrassed, so to break the tension and put him at ease, she turned to the others and asked, "What was it we were talking about?"

"The doctor was explaining why he's headed to Durango," Arvis recalled.

"Yes, I was telling you about my daughter," Josiah said. "Laurel really is quite well educated. She has attended mission schools, and I made certain that there was always a steady stream of books delivered to the reservation. . . ."

As Josiah continued his story, Stephen settled back on his seat and accepted his wife's hand. He slowly forgot the disturbing images he had dreamed and found himself listening avidly to Josiah's recitation about Laurel's education and training as a physician.

". . . So after seven years studying and training with

me, I realized that she was fully qualified to practice medicine. All that remains is for her to prove her skills and receive her degree. And what better place than my old alma mater, Geneva Medical College? They have a wonderful one-year program that leads to the awarding of a doctorate in medicine.''

"But a woman?" Sadie asked in amazement. "An Indian woman, no less. I've never heard anything so preposterous.''

"Not in the least," Josiah replied, disregarding her disparaging tone. "All that is required is that a candidate for a medical degree be fully trained by a physician, then participate in a course of study to confirm their abilities. Laurel is more than qualified, and if she can pass the examinations, there is no reason why she should not receive her doctorate.''

"But a *woman*?" Sadie repeated. "A woman doctor? There's no such thing.''

Rebecca leaned forward and stared down the bench at Sadie. "Quite the contrary, Mrs. Goode. I am certain I have read of women doctors in New York City. Isn't that right, Dr. Fox?''

"It certainly is. And it all began with a classmate of mine named Elizabeth Blackwell. She overcame a lot of prejudice to gain entry to our class of '49, and from what I've heard, she's developed into a top-notch physician— the first woman to be awarded a medical degree in the United States. Today there are quite a few, and I'm determined that Laurel will be among them.''

"But even so," Sadie continued, "who will she doctor? Who in their right mind would place their life and health in the hands of a woman?''

"We do exactly that when giving birth," Merrilee reminded her, then seemed somewhat embarrassed by having spoken so boldly in front of men.

"Mrs. Davis is right," Rebecca said, taking up the

argument. "For countless centuries, women have been trusting other women when they give birth, so why not for other health needs? Does bringing a baby into the world require any less knowledge and skill than prescribing a fever reducer?"

"It's not the same," Sadie argued, waving decisively at the air around her. "It's a woman's place to do the nursing, while doctors decide what kind of nursing a patient should get."

Rebecca noticed the way Arvis nodded his head in blind agreement, and it struck her that everything Sadie Goode was saying belied her own domineering relationship with her husband.

Suddenly Sadie leaned forward and addressed Stephen. "Mr. Davis, give us a man's opinion on this subject. Surely you agree with me."

Stephen eyed Sadie curiously, then turned to his left and stared for a moment at Josiah Fox, who seemed genuinely eager to hear what the young man had to say. "I really haven't given the subject much thought," he tentatively began.

Sadie looked a bit exasperated. "You'd certainly give it thought if *you* had a daughter who announced she wanted to be a doctor. Just imagine that! I have no doubt you'd set her straight—and fast."

"But if she really had the desire and talent . . ." Stephen's voice trailed into thought, then he turned to Josiah. "I mean, you did say there are women doctors today."

"You can't be serious!" Sadie exclaimed.

Without responding to her, Stephen continued to address Josiah. "There was a time when I wanted to be an artist. But of course that was different. Father was right in forbidding such a romantic notion. After all, there really is no future in art."

"And what kind of future would there be if all the

doctors and soldiers and politicians were women, while the men stayed home to clean the house and cook?'' Sadie persisted, though she had lost her intended audience. Stephen had leaned back against his seat and was lost in thought.

What kind of a future? he wondered. What would happen if all the old values were overthrown and people were left to devise new ones of their own? Indeed, wasn't this process already happening? Wasn't this very journey, sharing a stagecoach with a half-breed and a former slave, evidence of how severely unraveled the fabric of society had become? Sadie Goode was right. Being an artist was better left to dreamers who did not have families or real responsibilities, just as doctoring was best handled by men.

Stephen Davis shook himself out of his stupor and sat up straighter. ''You are perfectly right, Mrs. Goode. People should remember their proper place in life—and not just women.'' He shot Tom Kennedy a withering look.

The temperature fell considerably during the next hour, and now several of the passengers were bundled in thick wool blankets provided by the stage line. Conversation dropped to a minimum, consisting of little more than a periodic polite apology when the sway of the coach caused one person to bump another too roughly.

Rebecca Williman pulled her blanket tighter around her neck as she leaned back and closed her eyes. Though she remained fully awake, pictures began to come unbidden into her mind's eye, fashioned by the light that danced across the surface of her eyelids from the oil lamp beside her.

At first the random visions were warm and inviting: candles on a birthday cake, the family gathered around a bonfire after a winter sleigh ride, her mother smiling at her from in front of a glowing hearth. Flooded with a sense of well-being, Rebecca pulled the images to her and let them warm her from within. But as she gazed lovingly upon these radiant scenes, they began to fade, and she felt a foreboding chill course through her body.

Rebecca tried to call out for her mother, but the woman's features became blurred and indistinct. The figure approached from in front of the hearth, and with a start Rebecca realized the woman had transformed into her father. He loomed above her, stern and unyielding, his arms raised not to caress, but to strike. Then he began to recede toward the flames beyond, until with arms outstretched and beseeching, he entered the blazing fury and was consumed.

As the flames leaped higher, Rebecca grew colder. The fire was all around her now, lapping at her feet and hands and face, turning her blood into ice. She could feel a raging scream building in her throat, her entire being crying out for her father. But no sound would come. She could hear him calling to her, begging forgiveness and pleading for her to deliver him from the fire. But though the flames were all around her, they seemed unable to touch her. And so she grew colder, listening to her father's anguished cry, surrounded by his death pyre, but curiously— and painfully—detached.

Just then a voice called through her dream: "Rebecca, won't you step outside also?"

She opened her eyes to see Quint Burgess standing in the open doorway looking up at her. Beyond him, the rest of the passengers stood huddled in the darkness.

"Why, yes, of course," she replied as she accepted Quint's hand and stepped from the coach.

Rebecca noticed that it was snowing lightly as she approached the other passengers and looked around for the way station. But there was nothing but trees and snow. She stared back at the stagecoach and noted for the first time the curious angle at which it sat.

"What happened?" she asked Merrilee, who was standing nearby.

"The driver says that awful jolt was caused by a log. Apparently the horses spooked at some animal—probably little more than a rabbit."

"And the snow?" Rebecca asked.

"It's been coming down for over an hour," Merrilee said. "But he doesn't think it will amount to much. It's only October. Also, we're not far from the next station."

Rebecca stood and watched as Quint examined one of the front wheels. She was amazed that she had not felt the collision and realized she had indeed fallen asleep.

"I'll need you men to help hoist the coach," Quint called over to the passengers. "The hub pin came off, and I've got to reset the wheel."

Tom Kennedy immediately headed over to the coach, with Arvis Goode starting after him. But Sadie pulled Arvis back and whined, "You'll do no such thing. We're paying customers, not hired hands."

As Quint stood waiting, it became apparent that Stephen Davis also had no intention of assisting, so he called out, "That's okay with me, but you folks may not enjoy spending the rest of the night in the snow."

Flashing a look of annoyance at the other men, Josiah Fox stepped forward. "I'd be most willing to help you, Quint," he offered.

That seemed to do the trick. Stephen quickly said, "That won't be necessary, Mr. Fox. We can handle it," and headed over to the coach. Likewise, Arvis pulled away from his wife and joined the other men.

Under Quint's supervision, the men lifted the axle while Quint worked the cumbersome wooden jack. Once the coach was raised on the jack, the four men pulled off the wheel so that Quint could clean and grease the axle. Finally they hoisted the wheel back up and began to work it into position. All went smoothly until Stephen slipped in the slush, letting go of the wheel. It toppled to the ground, banging into Kennedy and staggering him backward.

"Dammit man, be more careful," Kennedy muttered as he rubbed his side where the wheel had struck.

"Me?" Stephen said, his eyes darting nervously from one man to the other, his look a mixture of embarrassment and outrage. "It's you who should be careful." He turned to Quint and Arvis. "Didn't you see the way he stepped in front of me and made me slip? I'm sure those footprints will confirm everything." He pointed to an indistinguishable jumble of prints in the snow.

"Just forget the whole thing," Kennedy declared as he pushed past Stephen and helped Quint and Arvis steady the wheel. "It was only an accident. No harm done."

"See that?" Stephen pressed with a smug smile. "He as good as admits it was his fault."

Kennedy glowered at the young southerner but held his tongue. Quint was not as gracious.

"All that I see," Quint announced, "is a spoiled young man who damn well better get to work so we can get this stage rolling again." He put his shoulder to the wheel and glared at Stephen Davis. "Now, lift!"

Stephen approached and took his place at the wheel. As he helped lift it into place, he watched the black man straining beside him. And when Kennedy looked over at him, it was as if the black man's dark, accusing eyes were burning with the same hurt look of betrayal as when Stephen had pointed a finger at Willie and had watched his father drag his young friend away.

Chapter Five

The snowfall had stopped by the time the stagecoach reached the next way station, so Quint Burgess decided it was safe to continue to Durango as scheduled. The horses were changed and the wheel checked, and once again they were on their way. But an hour later, well after midnight, the storm began again in earnest, the wind raging. Despite the clouds and screen of snow, the full moon gave enough light to turn the forest into a fierce fairyland, through which the biting wind howled like a hungry pack of wolves.

"Better check Little Bear's line," Quint called over his shoulder to Lucas as the big dog pranced restlessly along the coach roof.

While the boy made sure the leash was fastened securely to the iron rail surrounding the roof, Quint turned to Laurel beside him and said, "Why don't I pull up, so you can join the others inside."

"Oh, no," she replied, "I'd much rather stay up here. I'm really quite warm." And indeed, she looked comfortable huddled in her fur-trimmed cloak beneath the bearskin rug Quint had given her. "But perhaps Lucas would prefer it below."

"No," Quint said quite emphatically. "He never rides in the coach, no matter the weather. He'd rather stay with me. It's been that way ever since his mother died. I think he's afraid of losing me, also.''

Laurel gazed at the handsome, blue-eyed stage driver, then turned to share a smile with his ten-year-old son, who was on the raised seat behind her. She noticed that Lucas's hair was lighter than his father's, and his features were softer and less sharply defined, but his smile was just as genuine and his gray eyes revealed the same compassion and uncompromising honesty.

Realizing Lucas did not rely on hearing to communicate, she shared a private thought with him by mouthing the words, ''I like you, Lucas.''

Seeming to understand, his grin broadened, and he opened his mouth as if to speak. His tongue and lips struggled, but no sound came. He looked down at his feet, his face flushed with embarrassment.

''You don't have to speak,'' Laurel said aloud as she reached over and touched his chin in an attempt to regain his attention. But Lucas abruptly jerked his head away and scuttled across the bench to a safer position behind his father.

Quint seemed aware of the interplay. ''It's not you, Laurel,'' he reassured her. ''I told you that Lucas has been a bit withdrawn since his mother died. I also should have told you that somehow it put a wall between him and women. He seems afraid of their touch. I guess it reminds him of his mother—of what he lost. It used to bother me, but I've decided it's best not to make too much of it. I think it will pass. In fact, I'm sure it's beginning to already. He certainly likes you. I saw the way he gave you that apple.''

Quint turned on the seat and tousled his son's hair. ''I was real proud of you, son, for doing that.''

Lucas seemed to understand he was being praised, and he smiled at his father.

Realizing Lucas's head was uncovered, Quint added,

"But get your hat on, or I'll be more than proud to wallop you one!" To drive home the point, he forcefully gestured at the hat on his son's lap.

Lucas clapped the hat on his head. Then in retaliation, he mussed up his father's uncovered hair. As Laurel and Lucas burst into laughter, Quint sheepishly picked up his own hat from the floor of the boot and put it on.

Laurel scanned the landscape through the screen of snow. They were coming down a long wooded grade, and the horses were having to pick their way carefully through the quickly mounting drifts.

"We didn't expect snow," Laurel told Quint as she looked out across the drifts. "We thought it would only rain."

"That's likely all they're getting back at the reservation," Quint replied. "The snow is probably just here in the high country. That's why I'm pushing forward. It's all downhill from here, and it won't be long before we cross the Animas River and reach the next way station. It might only be raining there right now. If not, we can wait at the station for the weather to clear. Then it's just a few hours to Durango."

The heavy snowfall and the crowding trees made visibility quite poor. But Quint knew every inch of the road, and he slowed the horses as they continued down the incline toward a sharp bend ahead. It was not until they were into the turn that Laurel realized it was there, and she marveled at Quint's expertise with the reins. Even at a crawl, the stage tipped sharply to the left; any greater speed would have resulted in disaster.

Suddenly Quint was sawing at the reins, pulling the four-horse team to a shuddering halt. Laurel grabbed the side rail to maintain her balance, and she prayed her father below had not been too badly jostled. The unexpected action was punctuated by a sharp bark from Little Bear, who would have slid off the roof if not for the restraining line.

"Fallen tree," Quint explained as Laurel turned to ask him what had happened. "See, just ahead." He pointed into the darkness beyond the horses, where a large tree trunk blocked the path.

"Must have been the wind," Laurel suggested.

Quint nodded absently, his eyes cautiously surveying the scene. Then he noticed the jagged marks of an ax at the base of the tree. He cursed abruptly and dove for the shotgun at his feet.

"Hold it right there!" a harsh voice demanded. Then, like apparitions in a dream, two riders materialized out of the gloom, their Winchester rifles trained on Laurel and Quint. The dream became a nightmare when Laurel recognized the men who had caused such trouble at the reservation way station. As the men pulled closer to the stage, Little Bear realized who they were, and he began a deep-throated growl.

"Just ease it down," the smaller man ordered Quint, whose shotgun was half raised by now.

When Quint hesitated, the fat one kneed his horse closer to the stage and pointed his rifle directly at Laurel. "My partner said to drop it . . . on the ground."

Quint tossed the shotgun into the snow beside the front wheel.

"That's better," Custer Vance said with a smirk. "Now spread that coat."

Quint did as told, revealing that he was not wearing a holster. Meanwhile, Little Bear sensed the danger to his friends, and his growl intensified, his lips curled back to bare his teeth.

"Shut him up—or I'll shoot him!" Vance demanded.

Quint turned in his seat and nodded at Lucas, who wrapped his arm around Little Bear to quiet him.

With a smug grin, Vance pulled back from the driver's

box and rode beyond Laurel to the coach door. At the same moment, the leather window curtain was yanked back, and an annoyed Sadie Goode stuck her head out.

"What's going on? You could have—" Her words were cut short by the rifle barrel that suddenly appeared in front of her nose. Beyond the barrel, she saw the big, slovenly man who had shared dinner with them, his meaty face split with a repulsive sneer.

Mustering a surprising amount of self-control, Sadie asked, "What's the meaning of this outrage?"

"Get the hell out of there," Vance barked in reply.

The other curtains were opening now, and Vance waggled his rifle at the rest of the occupants. "Get out! Everyone!"

As the passengers began to file out, Quint turned to Ned Purvis, who was still covering him with his rifle. "I don't know what you think you're doing," Quint said, "but you've made a big mistake. There's nothing of value on board. We don't even carry a strongbox."

"I'll decide what's of worth," Purvis replied. "And from what I saw at dinner, I'd say there's enough on board to make this little party worthwhile." He turned to Laurel with a lecherous smile. "Ain't that right, pretty half-breed?"

Laurel could feel Purvis's leering eyes burning through her, and she fought the urge to flinch. Her left hand moved a few inches along the seat and found Quint's, and in his firm grip she felt a renewed strength. As her body filled with that energy, she stared straight back at Purvis and concentrated on steadying her emotions. She would display no fear to this odious little worm and his fat, unkempt partner.

By now all the passengers had disembarked and were standing side by side in the snow, with Custer Vance covering them on horseback with his rifle. Ned Purvis thrust his own rifle back in the saddle scabbard and drew his revolver. He dismounted, removed the large saddlebag from his horse, tossed it over his shoulder, and approached the stagecoach.

Purvis moved from one passenger to the next, checking to make certain no one was carrying a weapon. All but Tom Kennedy were unarmed, and Purvis almost missed his gun—an ivory-handled, short-barreled revolver in a shoulder holster.

"Pretty fancy rig for a nigger," Purvis declared as he yanked the gun from Kennedy's holster. "Steal it off a white man? Maybe this pretty boy over here?" He nudged Stephen Davis with the butt of Kennedy's revolver, then shoved the gun in his own waistband. "Oh, I forgot," he said, turning to address the young southerner. "Your pappy probably don't think you're old enough to carry a man's weapon, like the nigger."

His anger flaring, Stephen took a step forward and said, "Look, mister, you've got no call to talk to us—"

With the speed of a striking snake, Purvis smacked Stephen across the face with the back of his hand. Without a word, he turned and walked back down the line of passengers, leaving Stephen to rub his stinging cheek.

"Now open up them pockets and purses and fill this bag," Purvis ordered as he holstered his revolver and held forth the saddlebag.

One by one, the passengers complied, prodded now and then by the outlaw when he thought they were holding back or moving too slowly. When he came to Merrilee Davis, he did not wait for her to remove her pearl necklace and gold brooch but simply snatched them off her, tearing a ragged hole in her fawn-colored dress. He gave a sideways glance at Stephen, as if challenging him to interfere. Then he turned back to Merrilee and demanded, "The rings, too." Tears flooded Merrilee's eyes as she removed her engagement and wedding rings and added them to the saddlebag.

When Purvis had gathered all the jewelry and billfolds,

he tossed the saddlebag over his shoulder and headed back to his horse.

"What about the squaw?" Vance asked as his partner prepared to mount up.

Purvis looked at the driver's box, then over at Vance. "It's gonna be a cold night. Let's take her with us." He gave a short, gutteral laugh. Then he drew his revolver and pointed it at Laurel. "Climb on down from there, half-breed." Again Little Bear began to growl as he strained at the end of his leash. "And keep that damn dog on that line, or I'll let my friend empty that rifle into his damn hide!"

As Laurel gripped Quint's hand tighter, Quint leaned forward and said, "You're not taking anyone anywhere, mister. You've got what you wanted. Now move on."

"Not everything," Purvis replied. "And this revolver says I can take what I damn well please. Now get the hell down here, woman!"

A thin but firm voice spoke from beside Purvis: "She won't do anything of the kind."

Purvis spun around to see Josiah Fox approaching. "Get on back, old man," the outlaw demanded. "I'm taking her, and there's no need for you to die over it."

Josiah walked beyond Purvis and planted himself between the outlaw and the stage, some twenty feet away. "Laurel will not be taken anywhere against her will." His voice was calm and forceful.

"Is that so?" Purvis smirked. "And who's gonna stop me?"

Purvis roughly pushed Josiah aside and started toward the driver's box. But Josiah moved deftly in front of him again. Purvis lifted his arm and, with a look of boredom, struck the old man full force across the cheek with the barrel of his revolver. Josiah collapsed to his knees.

With a cry of alarm, Laurel clambered down from the driver's box, but she was met by Custer Vance, who had kneed his mount over to the front of the coach. The burly man leaned down from his horse, yanked back her hood, and grabbed hold of her long hair. With his other hand, he trained the barrel of his rifle on her temple.

Quint made a move toward the hidden Bowie knife in his boot, but Vance shot him a malevolent glare and said, "One more inch and I blow her away."

Seeing that his partner had things under control, Purvis started back to his horse. Unnoticed, Josiah Fox struggled to his feet. With faltering steps, he strode over to Purvis and grabbed his shoulder, swinging him around.

"You won't do this," Josiah said. "You'll have to kill me first."

Purvis stared at the man's bloody face for a moment. Then he shrugged, lifted the revolver, and struck Josiah across the other cheek, again knocking him down. "Leave it be, old man," he said to the crumpled form in the snow at his feet. "There's nothing you can do."

But again, incredibly, Josiah pulled himself to his knees and slowly stood back up, his face a bruised and bloody mass. He swayed slightly as he staggered toward Purvis. "I mean you no harm, young man," he said. "I forgive you, even. But you will not take this woman against her will. You will have to kill me first."

"Don't make me do it," Purvis declared, his voice somewhat unsteady now. His eyes quivered nervously, and his expression was pained, almost as if he regretted what he had done to the old man. For a moment, he raised his gun as if to strike Josiah for a third time. Then he thought better of it and merely cocked the weapon and pointed it at him. "Don't make me do it," Purvis repeated.

But Josiah continued forward, until the gun barrel was pressed against his chest. Then he started to reach for the outlaw's revolver.

Purvis's hand wavered for a moment, his eyes darting between Josiah's hand and bloody face. He began to squeeze the trigger, then muttered *"Damn!"* and for a third time laid Josiah out with the barrel of his gun.

Laurel shrieked, and Custer Vance yanked her hair brutally. Purvis stood staring at the motionless figure lying in front of him in the snow. He was about to turn away when Josiah began to move, straining to lift himself onto his elbows. Purvis stared incredulously as the old man raised his head and looked at him, his eyes imploring, his lips upturned in a small, compassionate smile. Then Josiah Fox's strength gave out, and he collapsed to the ground.

"Enough!" Laurel cried out, almost hysterical. "Leave him be. It's me you want, and you can have me—I'll go with you peacefully—if you'll just leave my father alone and let someone carry him into the coach."

For a moment, Purvis continued to stare at the unconscious old man. Then he pointed his revolver at Tom Kennedy and snarled, "Go ahead—get him inside." As Kennedy hurried over and grasped Josiah around the chest, Purvis added, "Just make sure you get right back out here, nigger!"

The outlaws paid little attention as young Lucas Burgess scrambled down from the driver's box and rushed over to help Kennedy, lifting Josiah's feet as Kennedy pulled him by the chest. Atop the coach, Little Bear strained at his line in an effort to follow, and Quint grasped his collar to hold him back.

With the saddlebag of valuables still over his shoulder, Ned Purvis sauntered to the front of the stage and began unharnessing the team of four.

"Now, just a minute—" Quint began, but Purvis cut him off with a scowl.

"I decide what happens here," Purvis declared. "And what I say is that we're taking the horses. Won't hurt you folks none to spend a night on the trail, and by the time you make it to the next way station, we'll be clean gone."

Purvis quickly freed each horse from the tongue of

the stage, attaching its lines to the next horse in the team.
Then he led the lead animal forward, with the other three
horses trailing behind. When the team was clear of the
stage, he dropped the reins of the lead horse and looked
back. Tom Kennedy had just reemerged from the coach,
while Lucas remained inside with Josiah Fox.

Purvis turned to his partner, who still held Laurel by
the hair with his rifle to her head. "C'mon, let's ride," he
called to Vance as he walked away from the stage team
and headed over to his own horse.

All this time, Sadie Goode had been slowly stepping
back, until she was mostly hidden from sight behind the
other passengers. Her eyes blazed with a bitter fury as she
saw these upstarts preparing to ride away with the riches
that were supposed to be hers. But now she saw an opportunity to turn this disaster to her own advantage, and she was
determined to see it through. She knew the time had come
for her to shake off the facade she had so carefully
constructed. The time had come to stop playing the fool.

Sadie reached down and lifted the hem of her dress.
Her other hand slid cautiously up along her leg, until she
felt the cool metal of the small Smith & Wesson that was
strapped to her thigh. She wrapped her fingers around the
mother-of-pearl grips, found the trigger, and drew the
weapon out.

From the corner of his eye, Ned Purvis saw the
matronly woman step swiftly into the open, her arms
raised and steadying something black and ominous in her
grasp. He had no time to react before the object belched
fire. An explosion shattered the night as a flash of searing
heat tore into his thigh.

With a cry of pain, Purvis stumbled to his side,
crashing against his horse. The animal reared up and bolted
into the darkness, causing Purvis to collapse to the ground.
The action saved his life, as Sadie's next shot whistled
past his head.

Custer Vance let go of Laurel and raised his rifle toward the passenger with the gun. But the rifle was barely up when a furious black cloud came hurtling at him from the roof of the stage. Quint had released Little Bear's collar, and the huge dog sailed through the air and landed on Vance's back, knocking him off balance. The fat man screamed as Little Bear's teeth sank into his shoulder, yet he managed to hold onto the saddle, though not without dropping his rifle. As Vance almost fell to the side off the saddle, the weight of Little Bear caused the animal to go toppling to the ground, taking a generous hunk of Vance's skin in the process.

Before Little Bear could recover and attack again, Vance struggled upright and put his spurs to his horse's sides, turning the animal and racing over to his wounded comrade. Purvis had somehow managed to get to his feet, and he reached out eagerly and vaulted up behind Vance. The big man drew his revolver now and turned toward the stage, trying to steady his horse so that he could shoot. Nearby, the stage horses tugged frantically at one another but held their ground.

Quint Burgess had already leaped from the box, and he snatched up the shotgun he had been forced to throw down. From behind the front wheel, he raised it and squeezed the trigger, but at the last second he yanked the barrel upward, and the shot went into the air. A dark form had appeared directly between him and the outlaws. It was Laurel, who had retrieved Vance's Winchester and was now preparing to return his fire.

As Vance began to shoot wildly at the passengers, he found himself facing a hail of bullets from Laurel's rifle. Cursing, he turned his horse and galloped off into the night, with Ned Purvis hanging desperately to him, shouting, "The bag! Dammit, I dropped the bag!" Vance paid no attention to his partner but spurred his horse all the faster, his eagerness to escape fueled by the second barrel of

Quint's shotgun, which exploded now from the darkness behind him.

As the outlaws disappeared into the night, Quint dropped his gun and hurried over to Laurel's side. Nearby, Arvis Goode stood in shock, staring disbelievingly at his wife.

With a firm stride, Sadie stepped over to her husband and shook him. "This is our chance!" she whispered. When he did not respond, she shook him again and said, "The bag! Go get the saddlebag!"

She pointed toward the dark object that was lying on the ground near where Ned Purvis had been shot, then shoved Arvis toward it. He took a few uncertain steps, turned to his wife, then seemed to get a grip on himself and hurried over to the bag of valuables.

Nearby, Quint held Laurel in his arms. Her body was trembling slightly, though more from relief than from fear. Then she suddenly pulled away from Quint and cried, "My father!"

She turned and found herself facing Sadie Goode, who still held the Smith & Wesson in her hand. "Thank you," she whispered as she started past Sadie toward the stage.

"Not just yet," Sadie said in a strikingly resolute voice.

"What?" Laurel asked.

"Your father can wait a minute. You and that driver just walk over to the other passengers, real slow and easy."

For a moment Laurel and Quint merely stared in wonder at her. Then as Sadie backed over to where her husband was standing, they realized the revolver was pointed at them in a more than casual fashion.

The other passengers started forward, and Sadie waved the gun at them. "All of you, just stay where you are. There's still plenty of bullets in here."

"What the hell are you doing?" Quint asked.

"I'm sorry to have to do this, but my husband and I are taking over where those two jokers left off." To their incredulous stares, she added, "You don't think I risked my neck for that costume jewelry I was wearing? No, I did it for these." She leaned over and shook the bag in Arvis's hand. "That's why we boarded this stage in the first place, only now those two fellows already did the hard work for us. Oh, yes, I'm afraid we'll have to take those horses, also."

Sadie nudged her husband toward the string of horses, which were still stirring restlessly. Just then she saw that Ned Purvis's horse had wandered back and was stamping nervously in the snow nearby. "You take the stage team, and I'll ride that one over there," she told Arvis, who seemed uneager to comply. "Well, get going," she insisted.

"Couldn't we leave them a couple?" he asked nervously. "We shouldn't abandon them in this snow-storm without a horse."

"Idiot!" she shot back. "Leave them just one and it won't take but an hour for them to have a posse on our trail. We take them all, or we might as well take none."

Quint stepped forward cautiously. "You can't seri-ously be planning to leave us out here like this. There's a good foot of snow on the ground, and it'll be worse before the night is over."

"You'll be all right," Sadie muttered as she backed over to Purvis's horse and grasped the reins.

"But my father . . ." Laurel pleaded.

"He's just bruised."

"He is an old man," Tom Kennedy said, walking over to where Laurel and Quint were standing. "And he's sick. You heard the way he was coughing in the stage."

As Sadie mounted the horse, she waved away the comment with an annoyed frown. "I said we're taking the horses. The old man will be just fine. He's a doc, right?

He knows how to take care of himself. Hell, he's only shaken up a mite.''

Arvis climbed up on the bare back of the front horse in the string and tightly clutched the harness collar. With her gun still carefully trained on Quint and the others, Sadie kneed her horse over beside Arvis and yanked the saddlebag from his shoulder, slinging it across the saddle in front of her.

''Now, we're going to ride out of here real peaceful-like, and in the morning one of you folks can mosey on back to the last way staion and bring along some new horses.'' She pointed at the shotgun and rifle lying in the snow near Quint. ''I want you to pick those up by the barrel, nice and easy, and toss them over into the trees. You can get them back after we're gone.'' As Quint complied, she added, ''See? I'm not so heartless, after all.'' Then she turned her horse and led the way north along the snow-covered stage road. Behind her, Arvis struggled furiously to keep the stage horses moving and in line.

As the sound of the horses' hooves thudding in the snow receded, the stillness was shattered by the short, piercing wail of a child, followed by a series of long, wrenching coughs. Laurel raced to the coach, threw wide the door, and looked inside.

Lucas was huddled in the far corner, his knees drawn up to his chest, his eyes opened wide in horror. Across the aisle on the rear bench, Josiah Fox was lying in a pool of blood. His body quivered as each racking cough ended with a gush of blood, which poured down his chin and soaked the front of his suit. As Josiah started to gag on the fluid, Laurel leaped into the coach and turned his head to the side, so that the blood would clear his throat. But the front of his suit continued to soak with fresh blood, which ran freely down his side and pooled on the floor of the stage.

Laurel pulled the flaps of Josiah's coat aside and tore open the vest and shirt. She wiped away the blood with her hand, but it kept coming. Then she saw the thumb-sized hole in the side of his chest. Ripping a clean swath of material from the bottom of the shirt, she balled it up and pressed it tightly against the wound. As it rapidly reddened and soaked through, she began to sob.

"My God," she gasped. "He's been shot!"

Chapter Six

Under Laurel Fox's direction, Quint Burgess and the passengers quickly transformed the interior of the stagecoach into a makeshift medical examining room. Josiah was semiconscious, stretched out on his back on the center bench, which Quint had opened to its full length. His coughing had subsided, and the flow of blood from his chest was being stanched by Tom Kennedy, who leaned across from the rear bench and pressed a large wad of cloth against the wound. Quint sat across from Kennedy on the forward bench, ready to assist as needed. Laurel and Lucas kneeled in the aisles next to the center bench, Laurel on Quint's side and Lucas by Kennedy.

The leather window curtains were drawn and tied, and the door at Josiah's feet was closed. At his head, however, the door was left open. Outside, a large blanket had been secured to the roof rail, and it hung down over that entire side of the coach. Standing beyond the doorway under the shelter of the blanket were the Davises and Rebecca Williman, with Stephen holding a lantern to better illuminate the interior of the coach. A second lantern was suspended directly above the center bench from one of the straps that normally held the removable backrest.

Laurel opened her father's black surgical bag, rummaged around inside, and produced a folded square of cloth, which she spread open on the rear bench beside Lucas. Then she searched through the bag again and removed a large leather bundle. After undoing the drawstring, Laurel carefully unrolled the packet, revealing an array of gleaming surgical instruments, each in its own pocket. She examined each one before finally selecting a slender knife, which she held out to Lucas.

"Scalpel," Laurel said, repeating the word as she handed the surgical knife to the boy, who hesitantly held out his hand to accept it. As she placed the handle in his palm, she made signs to show that he must not touch the end that would be used in the surgery. Lucas nodded his understanding, and his concentration was so complete that he seemed unaware that his and Laurel's hands were touching. After he inspected the instrument, she directed him to place it on the cloth she had spread on the rear bench.

"Forceps," Laurel continued, handing the second instrument to Lucas. Again he nodded and took it by the handle, then laid it on the bench alongside the scalpel. In like fashion she gave him a probe, a retractor, a needle holder, and a box of catgut ligature threads.

Laurel reached up and adjusted the wick of the lamp overhead. When her father suddenly moaned and stirred on the bench, she told Kennedy to ease the pressure on his chest slightly. Then she tenderly caressed Josiah's face and whispered, "It will be all right, Father. Rest now."

Laurel took a metal bowl from the surgical bag and placed it on the bench beside Quint. Next she found a bottle of antiseptic, unscrewed the cap, and half filled the bowl with the diluted carbolic acid. She placed the open bottle on the bench beside the bowl.

While working, Laurel dispassionately detailed each step of the procedure, more to keep her mind focused on her work than to educate the passengers about what she was doing. "New theories hold that hospital infections are often caused by contamination of the wound by the surgeon's instruments," she said. "It has been suggested that immersing the instruments in boiling water or in an antiseptic such as this carbolic acid can greatly reduce such risk."

Laurel turned to Lucas, who looked at her expectantly from the opposite side of the center bench. "Probe, Lucas. Give me the probe." The boy's expression took on a mixture of uncomprehension and fear. "Give me the probe, Lucas," she repeated.

When the boy again did not respond, Rebecca Williman leaned into the stage. "Laurel, perhaps I should do that for you," she offered. "He doesn't understand, and he must still be upset about—"

"No," Laurel abruptly cut her off. "It is important that Lucas participate. If he sees what is going on, he will not be so frightened. He was alone in here when Josiah was shot, so he may feel somehow responsible. If he assists, it may ease any misplaced sense of guilt." She glanced at Quint, and he nodded his support.

Laurel turned to Lucas again and asked for the probe, holding her hand out. This time Lucas seemed to understand, and he turned to examine the array of instruments on the bench beside him. Correctly picking out the long, slender surgical probe, he handed it to her.

"Thank you, Lucas," she said with a warm smile.

Laurel dipped the probe into the bowl of antiseptic and asked Kennedy to remove the bandage. As he lifted the cloth from Josiah's chest, Laurel saw that the flow of blood had largely stopped. It renewed slightly when she inserted the tip of the probe into the thumb-size entry hole of the bullet.

As she began to examine the wound, Josiah moaned and stirred fitfully. "Hold him steady," she instructed, and Kennedy and Quint each took hold of one of Josiah's arms.

Laurel worked quickly and expertly, and after a few

moments she removed the probe, wiping it on a clean cloth and handing it back to Lucas. She turned to the others and shook her head in dismay.

"It is as I suspected," she grimly announced. "The bullet hit the edge of the sternum and was deflected, probably into the lower lung. I will have to open the chest cavity to remove it and repair the lung."

"But here?" Merrilee Davis asked incredulously. "In a stagecoach?"

"I wish it were otherwise, but there is no other choice."

Laurel bent over and looked through the surgical bag. Removing a small wooden box, she pried off the lid and reached inside. Cushioned in a roll of gauze was a tiny glass vial, which she withdrew and handed to Quint. Then she unrolled the gauze and placed it over her father's nose.

"That is chloroform, Quint," Laurel told him. "You must use it exactly as I instruct. The rubber cap protects a glass spout. When you remove the cap, you can turn the bottle over and administer the anesthesia drop by drop. On my command, you will place three drops on the gauze directly over Josiah's nose. No more and no less. Later, I will have you add more, one drop at a time. But only remove the cap when you are about to dispense the chloroform, then close it back up immediately. Understood?"

Quint nodded.

"Then give him the first three drops right now."

Quint unstoppered the bottle, held it over the gauze, and carefully administered the anesthesia as directed. Laurel waited a few moments, listening to the change in her father's breathing. Then she leaned over and opened one of his eyelids, checking the pupil. Satisfied, she held her hand out to Lucas and requested the scalpel. He quickly responded and handed her the proper instrument.

Laurel immersed the knife in the antiseptic for a moment and then held it above her father's bare chest.

Turning to Tom Kennedy, she asked, "Could you keep the surgical area wiped as clear of blood as possible?"

Kennedy picked up a wad of cloth and nodded.

As Laurel made the first incision, Merrilee Davis shuddered and turned away from the sight of cold metal slicing through warm flesh. But as the operation progressed, she found herself irresistibly drawn to what was going on in front of her. She marveled at the skill with which Laurel worked, cutting through layers of tissue and working around the bone until she found and extracted the slug. Merrilee glanced at her husband and saw that he was just as fascinated with the entire procedure.

Stephen Davis flinched involuntarily as Laurel repositioned the retractor to open the incision wider and gain better access to the lung. But the rough jerking of the damaged tissue had no effect on Josiah, who appeared to be sleeping peacefully. On Laurel's command, Stephen held his lantern closer to better illuminate the interior of the wound, and as he stared into the gaping hole, he suddenly felt as if somehow he were intruding into the old man's very soul.

"This is a Hagedorn's surgical needle," Laurel explained as she placed a curved needle in the needle holder. "Formerly needles were triangular, like miniature bayonets. This flat needle has a cutting edge along one side, so that it makes a tiny slit, rather than a hole. When the thread is pulled and tied, it will effectively close the slit."

Threading the needle, Laurel continued, "I am using catgut thread—a relatively new procedure developed in England—which allows us to cut the sutures short and close the wound over them. The catgut will dissolve, and there will be no need to remove the thread, which used to be a common cause of infection and death."

Again Laurel adjusted the retractor that held the wound open. Then she leaned forward and checked Josiah's pupils.

"One more drop," she said, and Quint administered another dose of chloroform.

Laurel waited a moment, then began to suture the lung. Afterward she irrigated the interior of the wound with the diluted carbolic acid antiseptic as a further precaution against infection, then removed the retractor and sewed closed the entry wound itself. She thoroughly washed the surface of the wound in the antiseptic and finally covered the area with a gauze bandage.

Laurel removed the chloroform-soaked gauze from her father's face and leaned back with a sigh. "It is finished," she muttered.

"Will he be all right?" Rebecca asked.

"Only time will tell," Laurel replied, looking from one person to the next. In turn, they stared at one another, each of their expressions mirroring the wonder in their fellow passengers' eyes.

"I have never seen anything so remarkable before," Quint quietly intoned.

"And by a woman doctor," Merrilee added.

"It is nothing either of you women couldn't do with the proper training," Laurel said, "and with such capable assistance." She turned to Lucas Burgess. "Thank you so much for helping."

As she smiled, she took his hands in her own. Lucas pulled back slightly, suddenly afraid of her touch and yet mesmerized by this unusual woman all the same. Patiently, Laurel lifted the young boy's hands to her lips and kissed them. Slowly his body relaxed, and Lucas returned her smile.

While Laurel began to assemble her instruments and load them back into the large surgical bag, Tom Kennedy opened a wool blanket and covered Josiah Fox, who continued to sleep peacefully. "Is there anything else we can do for him?" Kennedy asked.

"He will probably sleep the rest of the night, which is

what he needs most right now. There was considerable damage to the lung, but I believe I stopped all the bleeding. Of course, that beating will complicate matters—and you probably noticed that he has tuberculosis. But Josiah is strong, and he won't leave us before his Lord decides it is his time. For now, it's best that he rest undisturbed. In the morning we can get him to Durango, where proper medical attention can be provided.''

Quint Burgess stepped outside and removed the large blanket canopy from the side of the stagecoach. Then everyone reboarded the coach, with Rebecca and the Davises on one bench and Kennedy and Lucas on the other. Laurel sat on the center bench with her back to the door and her father's head cradled in her lap.

In a moment Quint returned, his arms loaded with blankets from the rear boot, which he handed out to the passengers. Then he disappeared for a minute and reappeared in the doorway across from Laurel with a lantern in one hand and the shotgun in the other. Little Bear stood beside him, peering expectantly into the coach.

''Plenty of room on this side,'' Kennedy said, sliding over to make room for Quint.

''Not for me,'' Quint replied. ''The snowfall seems to be slowing, so I think I'll walk back to the last way station. It's only about five miles up the trail.''

''You're crazy,'' a stunned Stephen Davis said.

''I've got a good lantern,'' Quint replied, then tried to summon a smile as he added, ''and it feels as hot as a Georgia summer in this bearskin coat.''

''Wouldn't it be wiser to wait until dawn?'' Laurel asked, her eyes betraying her concern. ''Or at least let one of us go with you?''

''I can't allow that. This coach is my responsibility.'' He paused, looking from Laurel to her unconscious father. ''So is what happened to your father.''

''No one bears that kind of burden,'' Laurel insisted.

"Your only responsibility now is to see to the welfare of your passengers as best you can—which includes making sure that nothing harmful befalls their driver. Why not wait until morning, Quint," she added softly, but she could see that his mind was set.

"I should be back with fresh horses by dawn. There's more lamp oil in the compartment under the rear bench, as well as another canteen of water." Quint stepped up onto the iron foot rail and leaned over to his son. "Lucas, I am going for the horses," he carefully pronounced. "You stay here, all right?"

For a moment the young boy did not seem to comprehend, but when his father repeated the instructions, Lucas nodded his head. Then his eyes eagerly sought Little Bear, who stood outside with his front paws in the coach.

Quint raised Lucas's chin so that he would see him speaking. "I am taking Little Bear with me."

Again Lucas nodded, and this time he looked somewhat reassured, as if he knew nothing bad could happen with Little Bear along.

Quint stepped back down to the ground, raised his lantern, and looked a final time at the passengers. "I will return as quickly as I can," he said, his gaze finally resting on Laurel. Then he closed the stagecoach door and disappeared into a screen of snow.

Laurel watched until he was gone from sight. Then she closed her eyes and gazed into the distance. *"He'e'e' Ahi'ni'yo',"* she quietly intoned. "Walk with the Spirit."

To the north, Arvis and Sadie Goode were within three miles of the Animas River, beyond which the snowfall was already turning to rain. But they were unaware how close to salvation they were. Indeed, they had no idea where they were or even in what direction they were heading as the storm continued to rage about them.

To the west of the stage road, the forest had thinned

and eventually fallen away. Now, when the winds struck the timberline to the east, it deposited snow in ever higher drifts across the roadway. The horses were laboring with each step, their frantic whinnying adding an ominous undertone to the high-pitched shriek of the wind.

Arvis, leading the string of stage horses, still rode behind Sadie. Ahead, he could see the dim silhouette of his wife. Wrapped in Ned Purvis's saddle blanket, she looked like a great gray ghost as she furiously kicked and slapped her animal forward. Every time she cursed and struck the horse's rump, Arvis envisioned that vicious little highwayman laying another blow across poor Josiah Fox's cheek. And each time her horse dutifully raised a hoof and took another painful step, he saw Josiah struggle to his elbows and smile compassionately at his tormentor.

"Enough!" he finally shouted, but his voice was swallowed by the wind. *"Sadie! Enough!"*

When she did not respond, Arvis patted his own horse's neck and urged him forward. Their progress was aided by the path Sadie's horse was cutting through the drifts each time it dragged itself another step forward, and slowly Arvis and the stage team drew close.

"Sadie, wait up!" he called out, and this time she turned in the saddle and stared back at him.

"What is it?" she yelled, and as her attention shifted to Arvis, her horse came to a grateful halt.

Arvis pulled up and slipped off the lead horse's back. As he plowed forward through the snow, he realized it was almost two feet deep already.

"We can't go on like this," he began as he drew alongside of Sadie and grabbed hold of her stirrup.

"Don't be stupid, Arvis. Of course we can go on. We *have* to go on."

"We don't even know if we're still on the stage road," Arvis argued. "When we were in the woods, it was a clear path through the trees. But now it's an open plateau to the left. For all we know, the road could've veered off in that direction."

"Look, Arvis, get back on that horse and keep moving! We're bound to hit the river somewhere up ahead." The wind suddenly gusted, nearly drowning out her final words as she added, "You got a better notion?"

Still clutching onto the stirrup with one hand, Arvis bent over and pulled the collar of his too-thin coat tight around his ears. He was hatless, and his thin hair was caked with ice. When the gusting subsided somewhat, he looked up expectantly at Sadie and suggested, "We could follow our tracks back into the woods and return to the stagecoach."

"Don't be an ass!" she spat out. "What tracks? They get buried as fast as we make them."

Indeed, the wind already had filled with snow the last few steps Arvis had taken.

"All we have to do is follow the edge of the woods until we see the opening of the stage road," Arvis continued. "At least there'll be some shelter in the trees."

"We're not going back," Sadie replied firmly. "We'd probably get lost and be halfway to Utah before we realized it. No, we haven't turned off the road. We're still heading straight north. The trees just thinned out over there." She swept her arm across the barren plateau to their left. "We're going forward, and we're gonna make it. We *have* to. Did you see what those southern dandies stuffed into this bag?" She patted the saddlebag in her lap. "That Georgia snob must've been carrying a thousand dollars in his billfold—didn't even think to use a money belt! And those were real diamonds his prissy little wife was wearing. Now it's ours, and we're not gong back!"

"But Sadie—"

With an abrupt jerk of her leg, she pushed him away, then took up the reins. "Get on back to those horses.

We've gotta be long gone before they get that stage moving again.''

As Sadie began to knee her horse forward, Arvis reached out and yanked hard on the stirrup, forcing her to look back at him. "We're turning back, Sadie," he said with what seemed to be a firm resolve.

Sadie stared at him in disbelief, then shook her head as if dismissing a disobedient student. "Don't be stupid. I said to get back on your horse."

"No, Sadie, I won't. We're turning back. *I'm* turning back."

Suddenly Sadie began to snicker, at first softly, but then building into a deep belly laugh. "You, Arvis?" she finally managed to choke out as her laughter subsided. "You'd have to go back there without me, and you know you couldn't last five minutes on your own. You never could."

"I don't care anymore. I'm heading back, and I'm taking the horses."

"Damned if you do!" Sadie blurted out, furious now. "You can do whatever the hell you want, but I keep the saddlebag and the rest of the horses! You're not waltzing over there and handing back the stage team. Hell, they'd be on my tail in an hour! One horse, that's all you get, Arvis."

"I'm taking the whole team, Sadie. We never should have taken them in the first place."

Sadie squinted at Arvis, trying to read the thoughts behind his words. "So *that's* it," she finally said. "This whole thing has nothing to do with whether or not we're still on the stage road. You just feel sorry for those fools back there at the stagecoach." She sneered in disgust at her husband. "You lost most of your spine years ago, and damned if they didn't just take the rest of it!"

"You saw that old man," Arvis calmly replied. "He was beaten up pretty bad—and sick, too. He could die.

We're not murderers, Sadie. We never hurt nobody before.''

"*He* could die? What about me? Don't you care what becomes of me?''

"Of course I do, Sadie.'' He let go of the stirrup and eased his hand under the blanket and onto her leg, but she quickly slapped it away. "Come with me, Sadie. Let's do the right thing for once.''

"Hell, I don't know what's got into you lately, Arvis. You do what you think you must, but don't try to mix me up in your foolishness.''

Arvis stepped away from his wife. "I'm taking the horses, Sadie,'' he stated flatly. "All of the horses.''

Sadie looked at him intently and for the first time saw an unfamiliar flicker of strength. She shivered.

"You're getting soft, old man,'' she said, then glanced back at the string of four horses. "Go ahead and take the beasts, for all I care. You'll never make it back there, anyway, so it'll just be four—'' her gaze returned to her husband, who was shivering and looking very small in the snow "—make that *five* less animals for me to worry about. I've got what I want.'' She shook the saddlebag of money, then slapped the reins and started forward. "I've got what I want, and I don't need you anymore.'' She began to ride away. "And it won't be hard to find someone else to share it with.''

Arvis stared at her for only a moment before turning and heading back to the stage team. He hoisted himself up onto the back of the lead horse and kneed it forward.

Sadie glanced furtively over her shoulder and grinned in victory as her husband began to follow behind her. *He's so easy*, she reminded herself, and her smile slowly faded. *He was always so damn easy*. But her smile fell away completely as Arvis suddenly turned the animal in a wide circle and started back the way they had come, the rest of the stage team trailing obediently behind.

Sadie quickly pulled back on the reins and twisted in

her saddle. *"Arvis!"* she shouted. *"Come back this instant!"* But the only reply was the whistle of wind as her husband slowly receded into the storm.

"Arvis?" Her voice trailed off, and she sat staring in amazement as the last of the stage horses disappeared from view. It took a few more moments before she fully realized he was gone. Then she looked back at the saddlebag in her lap and swore under her breath.

"Damn that man!" Sadie muttered as she yanked the reins to the right, kicked her horse into a turn, and followed after her husband.

Chapter Seven

"**I** think he's finally asleep," Tom Kennedy told the other passengers as he patted Lucas's head.

The young boy was stretched out on the rear seat under several blankets, with his head on Kennedy's lap. Rebecca Williman sat across from Kennedy on the forward seat, with Merrilee Davis beside her and Stephen at the far end of the bench. Just across from Stephen on the center bench was Laurel Fox, still cradling Josiah's head in her lap.

"How is your father doing?" Stephen asked with a look of genuine concern.

"The chloroform must have worn off by now," Laurel replied, "but I don't believe Josiah will regain consciousness for quite a few hours."

"Is that serious?" Stephen asked.

"Actually, it's for the best. Sleep is the great healer—the best remedy for pain. If he awoke now, I probably would have to sedate him."

"He is such a brave man," Merrilee remarked. "You must be proud to have such a father."

Laurel nodded in agreement.

"I would only hope my father would find the strength to stand up for me the way yours did," Merrilee mused.

"But I am afraid there are few men who possess such unyielding courage."

Stephen repressed a grin. "Certainly not *your* father," he teased. "Martin makes even that meek Arvis Goode seem downright lionhearted."

"Now, you know that's not true, Stephen," she replied icily. "My father is just more sensitive than most men—certainly more than that despicable Arvis Goode character." She gave an involuntary shudder, as much from Stephen's assessment of her father as from the thought of the Goodes stealing their horses and valuables. Then she turned to Laurel and added, "My father is an architect. An educated man."

"An educated coward," Stephen said with a chuckle, then saw his wife's hurt expression and reached over to pat her hand. "I'm sorry, dear. You're quite right. Martin *is* a sensitive man."

Merrilee pulled her hand free and turned from her husband. "It's a quality I had once thought you to possess, Stephen."

"I'm sorry, Merrilee. But you know how it has always been for me." As Stephen continued, his gaze took in the rest of the passengers. "My father, Frederick Davis, is quite the opposite of Merrilee's. I suppose everyone considers Frederick to be the very personification of courage. He is one of the top fencing masters of Georgia, and he fought and won three duels before the Civil War. If at times I seem insensitive, it is because he insisted his children display the same iron will and determination, whether we possessed those qualities or not. There were no other choices for the children of Frederick Davis."

As Merrilee picked up the story, she took her husband's hand in her own. "Stephen has three sisters, but he's the only son," she said. "It was so much harder for him. And he *is* sensitive, I know that. My father is a great draftsman, but he says that Stephen is a true artist. He suggested that

Frederick send Stephen to Paris to study, but Frederick would have nothing of such a plan. Frederick raised Stephen to run a plantation, and there are no plantations in Paris."

"Don't be unfair to him," Stephen interjected. "He has always done what he thought was best."

"What *he* thought," she continued. "Never mind what you might think or want for yourself."

"But he was right—at least about my art. What kind of life would that be for a married man? What could it offer for you . . . and someday, for our children?"

Merrilee's voice was a whisper now. "I never asked for a plantation, Stephen. I only want you. And part of you is your art."

Laurel Fox leaned toward Stephen and asked, "Did your father-in-law stand up to Frederick about sending you to art school?"

"No one stands up to my father for long," Stephen replied grimly.

"I see," Laurel said thoughtfully, pausing a moment before adding, "That must have hurt deeply. You must have felt quite alone." Stephen was nodding slightly, staring vacantly at the floor. "But of course you didn't even try to stand up to him, Stephen, did you?"

"He was only eighteen," Merrilee explained.

"But nevertheless, you must have taken it as a sign of personal weakness, Stephen. No wonder you are impatient with weakness in others."

Stephen looked up at Laurel now, his eyes questioning.

"I think you are being far too hard on yourself," Laurel continued. "None of us is perfect. You must learn to forgive yourself, then you will be able to forgive Merrilee's father for failing to stand up for you. Finally, you must one day forgive your father for his constricting love."

At that remark, Tom Kennedy glanced over at Rebecca Williman, who was shifting uncomfortably on the seat. She caught his look and abruptly turned away.

"My wife is right about your father," Stephen softly told Laurel. "He is a very special man. I have never before seen such a selfless act of courage and love. I'm certain my father would have done *something* in the same situation, though not out of love, but hate. His actions would have stemmed less from concern for his child than from a sense that his personal honor was at stake. He probably would have gotten us all killed." He sighed. "Sometimes I wonder why I still love him."

"Don't be so rough on him," Kennedy interjected. "He's just a man, prone to the same hatreds as everyone else. When I was a boy—a slave boy—it was easy to hate. Every day we had a white devil to pin our hatred upon. And when we were freed from that living hell, we found it had been replaced with a new one, fashioned out of narrow-mindedness and bigotry—the kind that no proclamation will ever emancipate. Lincoln may have put an end to slavery, but my people still carry the chains in the color of our skin and in our hearts. So we slowly have become hardened, learning to return hatred with hate—until we end up despising what we have become. Then we must find a way to release that strangling hatred—or watch it destroy not only our enemies, but ourselves."

"That is a lesson my mother's people are also being forced to learn," Laurel said. "At one time, we were convinced we were a part of a holy war against the invaders of our land. Now that war is over, and we have lost. What once was a home without boundaries has been reduced to a reservation—a prison. There are those who want to rise up again and seek a noble death upon the bayonets of their enemies, while others worry that hatred will merely turn us into our enemies. It is a lesson taught by great peoples and nations, but which each person must learn alone."

"So each of us must learn to overcome the hatred within us," Kennedy continued. "It is a struggle I have fought these last sixteen years since Lee surrendered at Appomattox." As Stephen looked up at him now, the black man sensed that the young southerner was hearing him for the first time. "It is also a struggle *you* must face, Stephen," Kennedy cautiously added. "You are not your father. You can chart your own future. You can be the man you choose to be."

Kennedy saw how intently Rebecca Williman was looking at him, and he turned to her and asked, "Don't you agree, Rebecca? We need not be bound by our father's hatreds and sins. We are as free as we let ourselves be."

Rebecca bristled slightly, then said, "I can't fault your argument, Tom. But things are not as easy to act upon as they are to say. Surely you have learned that." She leaned forward and addressed the other passengers. "When Tom spoke to me of hatred and sin, he was referring to my deceased father, Hughes Williman. I think you would have easily recognized him, Stephen. Your father sounds so much like him. But Hughes was more than stern. He was cruel. I was his only family, so I bore the brunt of that cruelty, as did Tom Kennedy here. Yes, I admit that I hated him—indeed, I continue to hate him even now. And I can't wish away that hatred simply on account of a sentimental notion of compassion. I am a realist—too much like my father, I suppose. I hate him, and now he's gone. And the world is better for it."

"But don't you see that if he is gone, the only thing that remains is your hatred?" Laurel asked. "I would not presume to judge your feelings, but surely if the object has been removed, the hatred will eventually be directed at yourself."

"I'm sorry," Rebecca replied, "but I can't be theoretical about my feelings. I know the hatred is useless, but it remains, nonetheless."

"Your honesty does you credit," Laurel said. "Far more credit than my high-minded declarations do me." She looked down at her father for a long moment, tenderly touching his face. As she turned back to the passengers, her hands continued to caress his cheeks. "I can talk all I want about the need for forgiveness, yet I still feel a certain bitterness in my heart. I love Josiah dearly, and studying with him has been the greatest joy of my life. But I resent that I am unable to share my innermost thoughts and feelings with him."

"It is rare that a daughter can truly communicate with her father," Rebecca said.

"I can talk with him," Laurel continued, "but there are parts of my life I cannot share. You see, Josiah takes such pride in his medicine. He views the traditional Ute methods of healing as being based on worthless superstition, and he dreams of a new future for my mother's people. That is why I have never told him that I was secretly trained by the Ute medicine man Surnia."

"You are a medicine woman?" Stephen asked, aghast.

Laurel grinned. "I suppose you could call me that. At first I went to Surnia to learn more about my mother's heritage. Later I discovered that his medicine was based on a system of wholeness that is often lacking in European medicine. Our white doctors like to isolate and treat each part of the human body individually, as if the hand could live apart from the heart and lungs and brain. The Indian understands that all parts are interrelated, and so he treats the whole person."

"That may be so," Stephen admitted, "but he does it with useless herbs and roots and heathen incantations."

"Do not be so quick to reject an entire body of knowledge gained over hundreds of years of practical experience," Laurel cautioned.

"How did you keep your training a secret?" Merrilee inquired.

"My father's work took him all across the Ute reservation. There was ample time for me to visit Surnia and study with him."

"So you don't want to be a doctor?" Rebecca asked her.

"It is not that simple. I *am* a doctor—I am just not the doctor my father wants me to be. I have learned the ways of the white man and the Ute, and it is my dream to combine that knowledge and offer it to my people, who are in such need."

"Then why are you returning to the East?" asked Merrilee.

"Because my father wishes it. You have seen how frail he is. This dream is what keeps him alive, so I must go to New York and earn a piece of paper that is of no use to my people. And at a time when my skills are so badly needed."

"I assume you are referring to the relocation," Kennedy said.

"What relocation?" Stephen asked him.

"The Ute are being moved out of Colorado to new homes in Utah to make room for the miners and settlers," Kennedy explained. "I believe the tribes in the north are already on the move, and it is probably only a matter of time before the Southern Ute get moved, as well."

"Really?" Rebecca asked.

"As head of Williman Mining," Laurel replied, "I'd have thought you would know all about the forced migration. After all, Hughes Williman was one of the prime movers behind the plot to rob my northern brothers and sisters of their land—just as Williman Mining intends to steal my own reservation."

"Is this true?" Rebecca asked Tom Kennedy in astonishment.

"I'm afraid so," Kennedy admitted. "But surely you

were aware of your father's plans to mine the Southern Ute reservation.''

"Yes, of course, but nothing was ever said about kicking out the Indians.''

"Nothing ever *is* said,'' Kennedy noted. "It is just done.''

"Well, not as long as I am head of Williman Mining.''

"It may be beyond your control,'' Kennedy said. "Hughes Williman was just one player in a game that includes the army, the Congress, and many other mining companies.''

"So you see, Rebecca, my people need me now— not next year,'' Laurel continued. "If they are driven to Utah, the journey will be long, and many will perish along the way. Even now I should be traveling with the Northern Ute. It is said that scores already have died.''

"Then why don't you?'' Merrilee asked.

"Because of my father . . . and because of Surnia. Just as Josiah answered an inner call by coming to work with my people, so do I have a calling. Being half Indian and half white, perhaps I can help bridge the chasm between two great peoples. But as Surnia explained to me, as long as my father is alive, I must walk in his footsteps and pray the Great Spirit is guiding them. Such is the way of my people—the way I was raised. So I will fulfill my father's dream, even though I cannot share it.''

Josiah's head stirred slightly. His eyes opened, and he smiled. "Laurel,'' he whispered, his voice clear but exceedingly faint.

"Father!'' Laurel cried, bending over and kissing his forehead.

"You should have told me,'' Josiah said haltingly.

"Shhh,'' Laurel urged. "You must rest. Are you in pain? Do you need medication?''

"No, nothing. Plenty of time to rest later. Now you

must listen to me. You should have told me about your dream—about Surnia.''

"I am sorry, Father. I didn't want to hurt you.''

"But I was hurting *you*. I thought this journey was your dream, too. Forgive me for being so blind.''

"There is nothing to forgive, Father. Please don't talk anymore. You need to rest.''

"I will, Laurel, I will. But first you must do something.'' Josiah paused, then began to cough. A thin trickle of blood appeared at the corner of his lips. When the coughing subsided, he continued, "You must promise me that you will follow your own dream—that you will go wherever your voice calls, with my blessing.''

Laurel began to cry as she dabbed the blood from her father's face with a handkerchief.

"Promise me, Laurel.''

"I will, Father. I promise.''

Again Josiah began coughing, this time far more harshly. "Th-there is s-something else,'' he managed to stammer between coughs. "Something you must know.''

"It can wait,'' Laurel pleaded, wiping away the renewed flow of blood.

"No. You must be told. It is about Surnia.''

"Surnia?''

"I . . . I knew you were seeing him. I was too proud to let on that I knew.''

"But why?'' Laurel asked.

"I was afraid of losing you—like I lost your mother.''

"But she died in childbirth.''

"She wanted to give birth the old way—the Ute way. I wouldn't allow it. Insisted on performing the birth myself, without a midwife. But her people were not yet ready for anything like that. I didn't realize the shame it would bring her to have a man—especially her husband—in attendance during the birth.''

"It wasn't yor fault—" Laurel said, but was cut off by Josiah grasping her forearm.

"There's more," he said, his voice weakening. "With Surnia's approval, she concealed her labor and sneaked off to his cavern. There she had you alone, unattended even by Surnia. And she died."

"You didn't know," Laurel said, trying to soothe him. "It wasn't your fault."

"That was why I never allowed you to speak of Surnia. I was convinced I could have saved your mother, and I blamed him for her death. But even more deeply, I hated Surnia because, in your mother's time of need, she turned to her father instead of me."

"Her father?" Laurel asked, not understanding.

"Yes. Surnia is your grandfather. Forgive me for never telling you before."

"But Surnia never even hinted—"

"He accepted the will of his god. To him, by taking away your mother, the Great Spirit was commanding that you be raised by your white father. Surnia saw to it that no one ever told you the truth."

"And you knew I was training with him?" Laurel asked.

"Surnia first sought my permission."

"But why did you agree?"

"How could I stop you? If I had tried, I might have lost you forever. No, by then I knew that you must learn both paths if there was to be any hope of your choosing mine."

"And I do," Laurel said, hugging her father to her.

"No!" Josiah blurted out. "I was wrong to want you to choose. It was false pride. You are right—you must find your own path."

Josiah closed his eyes. His voice became so quiet now that Laurel had to lean close to hear. "My vision is much clearer now," he whispered. "There is nothing left to teach you. It is time for me to rest." Suddenly Josiah broke into a coughing spasm, and he clutched his bandaged chest. "It—it is t-time for me to rest."

As the gunshot wound ruptured, Josiah's lungs rapidly filled with blood. It sounded as though he were drowning as blood bubbled from his lips with each choking cough. With supreme effort, he opened his eyelids, and Laurel saw the growing glaze of death.

"No! Don't go, Father. Don't leave me!"

Josiah struggled to calm his heaving chest. When the coughing momentarily subsided, he smiled and haltingly said, "Your mother awaits me, Mountain Laurel, and she wants you to have her amulet." He started to reach for his neck. *"He'e'e' Ahi'ni'yo',"* he whispered. Then he was gone.

Laurel's tears flowed off her cheeks and mixed with her father's blood. "Walk with the Spirit," she intoned, closing his eyelids.

Lowering the blanket that had been covering him, she touched the small beaded charm that was fastened around his neck on a short leather thong. She carefully untied the thong and lifted the amulet—a bright yellow sunburst in a turquoise sky—which her mother had made for Josiah. As she held the amulet against her own throat and tied it in place, Laurel could feel her tears drying, her pain beginning to ease.

Josiah Fox's body was wrapped in blankets and carried by Tom Kennedy and Stephen Davis out into the storm, where it was tied securely to the roof of the stagecoach to await burial in Durango.

Three miles to the south, Quint Burgess was struggling toward the Durango Overland way station. Despite a thick bank of clouds, the full moon gave the landscape a soft glow, with Quint's lantern casting eerie shadows among the trees. The snow was so deep in places that Quint could see Little Bear only at the peak of each leap that the big dog made through the drifts ahead.

In his huge fur coat, Quint looked like a bear in a children's fairy tale, awakened from his midwinter slumber and, with lantern in hand, lumbering through the countryside in search of food. Little Bear was his faithful companion, scouting ahead to make sure no danger was lurking in the snowbanks.

As Quint plowed his way through the drifts, he found himself thinking of Laurel Fox. She was so different from the type of woman he had been attracted to since his wife's death. Rebecca, with her delicately applied makeup and flaming hair, far more closely fit the image. He had taken to letting physical attraction determine his interest in a woman, well aware that this was his way of avoiding any deeper involvement. But while Laurel was undeniably beautiful, it was a beauty that was inseparably related to her personality. What appealed to him was the complete woman, and it unnerved him.

There were many qualities in Laurel that reminded him of his dear Aileen—her natural beauty, her uncompromising courage and compassion, her intuitive understanding of others. But there were differences, as well. Aileen had been a woman of the city, never truly comfortable in wide open spaces. Such was the opposite with Laurel, whom Quint could not imagine serving tea in a New York City town house. And Aileen had been content with the role of wife and mother, whereas Laurel seemed unwilling to be bound by conventional restrictions.

But Laurel Fox was heading east to complete her training as a doctor. Afterward, she was committed to returning to the reservation and making a better life for her people. It was clear that there could be no future with such a woman—and Laurel was definitely the kind of person a man viewed in long-range terms. Far better to yield to an attraction with someone more firmly focused on the present—a woman such as the one she occasionally met in Farmington or Durango, who could help him ease his lonliness for a few hours, at least.

Quint nearly stumbled over Little Bear, who was standing still in the snow, his back arched and ears raised.

"What is it, boy?" he asked, leaning down and patting the dog's neck.

Little Bear began to growl softly. Quint steadied the shotgun under his left arm and took hold of the dog's collar. With his right hand, he raised the lantern to better light the trail ahead. It was then that he heard the wailing— not of the wind, but of an animal. The sound was picked up by others and turned into a howling chant: the cry of a wolf pack.

"Easy boy," he cautioned Little Bear. "It's just wolves. If you don't tangle with them, they won't bother with us. Anyway, I've got my shotgun."

The sound drew closer. Little Bear growled louder and began to strain at his collar.

"Take it easy," Quint repeated, pulling back on the collar. His words were as much for himself, for even though he had had considerable experience with wolves, such a howling never failed to chill his spine. "Wolves don't attack man," he reminded himself. "They avoid a fight and attack only the slowest and most sickly of creatures."

The pack was approaching quickly now. Quint raised the lantern higher and grasped Little Bear's collar more tightly.

"Indians call the wolf He-Who-Strengthens-the-Herd. They are God's winnowers, removing the weak and keeping the bloodlines strong."

It suddenly became silent, and Quint whispered, "See? They have seen us and will soon be gone. The snow hasn't been on the ground long—they can't be hungry enough for a fight."

Just then Little Bear gave a fierce tug, but Quint managed to hold onto him. Ahead, two eyes were illuminated by the lantern. Slowly a huge gray wolf came into view. The wolf glanced to the right, and following his eyes, Quint saw a half dozen other animals slipping out of the trees. An equal number now appeared phantomlike on the other side. But these were not wolves. They were wild dogs.

"Damn!" Quint cursed. He knew full well that a pack of wild dogs, even with a wolf leader, displayed few of the traits of a wolf pack. All he could count on was that they would be vicious. And indiscriminate. They would as soon attack a man as a deer—or even each other.

The dogs quickly surrounded Quint and Little Bear, their wolf leader standing aloof just beyond his circle of followers. One of the braver dogs slinked forward and took a tentative nip at Quint's heel, but was scared back by Little Bear, who spun around and growled sharply, nearly breaking free of his master's grip in the process. Quint clutched the collar more tightly, fearful that Little Bear would take on the whole pack and get himself killed.

The first dog was joined now by a second and third, and as the three of them cautiously approached, Quint began to wave the lantern in a wide arc to frighten them away. They darted back, but as soon as the lantern passed, they boldly came forward again, each time a step closer.

Little Bear was in a frenzy. Without letting go of the dog's collar, Quint placed the lantern in the snow and quickly shifted the shotgun to his right hand. He managed to cock one of the hammers, but as he lifted the double barrel to fire, a dog suddenly ran at him from behind, catching Quint on the calf and knocking him to the ground. The shotgun careened out of his hand, and as Quint grabbed for it, Little Bear broke free and leaped into the throng of wild dogs.

A sharp pain shot up his leg as Quint whirled around

and managed to shake off the dog. Just then another animal leaped at his throat. Quint instinctively raised his left arm, and the dog's teeth sank into the fur coat, which was thick enough to protect his skin. With the dog locked on his left forearm, Quint quickly slipped his right one around the animal's neck. He savagely yanked the dog's neck toward him and slammed the head back, instantly snapping the neck of the dog.

Quint tossed the dead animal into the pack, startling the other dogs and giving him enough time to stand. Yanking the bowie knife from his boot, he spun around just as another dog leaped at him. He lashed out and felt the knife go slashing through skin, and the dog yelped with pain and went darting away. Quint was immediately pounced upon by several more of the vicious animals, and the knife went flying from his hand. His heavy bearskin coat with its high collar protected his upper body, so his legs received the brunt of the attack, and again Quint was thrown to his hands and knees.

He had lost sight of Little Bear, but from the violent commotion nearby, he knew that his friend was bravely trying to protect him. Quint struggled to shake free of the wild dogs that leaped and tore at his coat. He finally gave up and attempted to curl into a ball to protect his exposed legs. The dogs seemed to sense his weak spot now and began to concentrate their attack on his legs. As Quint felt their fangs tearing into his flesh, he tried to crawl away, but he could not escape.

Just ahead of him in the snow was the lantern, and beyond it he could see the lone wolf staring at him, almost bemused. Quint pulled himself forward another foot, dragging the dogs behind, and reached out for the handle of the lantern. He snatched it up and swung it behind him, but the dogs were no longer afraid and continued to bite at his legs.

The ground began to roll beneath Quint; he felt as if

he were floating on the clouds. He knew he would soon be unconscious—then dead. His fingers were already becoming paralyzed, and he could barely feel the lantern in his grip. The darkness enveloped him, pierced only by two burning wolf eyes. They seemed to be taunting him, calling for him to give up this fight, as if the victory was complete.

Focusing all his consciousness into his right arm, Quint flung the lantern at those hypnotic eyes. There was a shattering explosion, and suddenly the eyes were ringed with a halo of flames.

As the lamp oil sprayed all over the wolf, it ignited and set his fur on fire. The dogs leaped back in fear, momentarily forgetting their quarry as their leader shrieked and howled with pain. The flames blazed upward, the fur sizzling and sparking as the wolf began to roll in the snow, dousing the fire.

Realizing he had but a moment to act before the flames would be out, Quint dragged himself across the snow and grabbed the barrel of the shotgun. As he lifted it from the snow, one of the dogs decided to return to his dinner and came at Quint's legs. Seeing him approach, Quint swung the shotgun and knocked the animal senseless with the butt. Then he flipped the weapon around in his hands and, leaning on it, forced himself to his knees.

The firelight flickered out as the wolf managed to douse the flames. He seemed more shocked than hurt as he leaped to his feet and howled. Then he came charging through his companions at Quint.

Raising the barrel of the shotgun, Quint pulled the right trigger and blasted apart the wolf and two dogs nearby. The rest of the pack darted away, then turned and stood staring at Quint and their fallen comrades. A few moments later, several of the animals came tentatively forward, sniffing at the wolf and staring at the tall man in the fur coat. Quint swiftly cocked the second hammer and fired. As two more dogs fell, the others turned en masse and raced away into the darkness.

Quint tried to stand, but his legs gave out, and he fell onto his stomach. He struggled to his hands and knees and looked around in the faint moonlight. Nearby he could make out a dark form stirring in the snow.

"Little Bear!" he cried, crawling over to his friend.

As he dragged himself through the snow, Quint could tell his legs were bleeding badly, but without the lantern it was too dark to assess the extent of his wounds. However, he realized he must do something to stop the bleeding, as well as to find shelter. But he felt so weak, and the ground continued to spin so rapidly around him.

Just need to rest a moment, he told himself as he pulled alongside Little Bear. The big dog was conscious, but whimpering with pain.

"We just need to rest," Quint whispered as he opened his bearskin coat and wrapped it tight around them both. Then he laid his head on the snow and closed his eyes.

Chapter Eight

Huddled in their thick woolen blankets, all but one of the passengers were asleep inside the stagecoach. Only Lucas Burgess was awake. He lay on the bench beside Tom Kennedy, his head on the black man's lap, his eyes examining each adult.

Lucas stared at the youngest of the men—the one with hair in ringlets the color of ripened wheat—who was leaning against the far corner of the coach. The boy's lips silently formed the word "Stephen" as he tried to distinguish the sound that invariably accompanied this word. As usual, the cacophony of noise that flooded his head all but drowned the individual sound of the young man's name. It had always been that way, with Lucas able to discern only fleeting strains of the music around him through the discordant rumble that continually thundered in his mind.

There was something about this elegantly dressed man that unnerved Lucas. At times his manner was so harsh and unpleasant, while at other times he seemed as friendly and gentle as Little Bear. Lucas had no idea how to approach or befriend him—always unsure if he would receive a smile or a snarl.

Slowly a tone surfaced in his consciousness and took form. *Eeevenn* the inner voice chanted as Lucas's lips slowly refashioned the blond man's name.

Leaning on the man's shoulder was a delicately beautiful young woman whose long, straight hair matched in color her husband's flaxen curls. As Lucas looked at her, he envisioned the fragile little china doll that used to sit on his mother's dresser. *Errrileee* his mind whispered as his lips formed her name. Lucas was not sure why, but he liked her—perhaps because she was the only one who consistently could soothe the beast that seemed to haunt her young husband.

Lucas turned to the corner directly across from him, where the woman with the flaming red hair was asleep. Her smile was always warm, and she was so pleasing to look at, but there was something in her nature that held people at bay—including Lucas. In sharp, staccato notes the word *Bekka* pattered through his consciousness several times, and Lucas grinned at the sound as he silently mouthed "Rebecca-becca-becca."

Looking up, Lucas watched Tom Kennedy's nostrils flare with each deep inhalation and felt his firm stomach expand and then contract, gently rocking the boy's head in his lap. Even asleep, the friendly man's face held a smile. The word *Tommm* rose effortlessly above the dissonance in Lucas's ears, followed by another remembered word: *friend*.

Lucas turned on his side now and hesitantly faced the woman who was lying alone beside him on the center bench. There was something of mystery to her—something totally captivating. Like steel to a magnet, he was drawn to her calm power and presence.

Aural, his mind intoned. *Aurrraaall*!

The woman with the long, free-flowing hair stirred, as if responding to his silent call. Then she settled back into the deepest of sleeps.

Ever so softly, Lucas whispered aloud, "Mama." Tears streaked his cheeks like the silver in Laurel's hair.

Lucas pulled his knees to his chest and held himself

in a ball. He tried to calm his body and still the harsh chorus of sounds that reverberated through him. But rather than relaxing, he suddenly felt very cold, as if the stagecoach had disappeared, exposing him to the bitter wind.

Above the wind, he caught snatches of a voice calling to him and briefly glimpsed his mother's face. Beside her was the kindly old man—Laurel's father—who had died on the very bench on which the Indian woman now slept. She had lost her father, as Lucas had lost his mother.

The faces faded away, and again Lucas felt himself lying in the snow. This time he was not alone; he sensed someone beside him. But it was no longer Tom Kennedy. It felt like a large dog, which was licking Lucas's face.

Lucas opened his eyes in sudden fear. He could discern the stagecoach and passengers, but with a shock he realized he could see right through them, as if that world was not reality but a specter—the stagecoach merely an image overlaid on the surface of another world, which was far more brightly illuminated and distinct. In this place where Lucas found himself, his blanket was transformed into a bearskin coat, and the black man beside him was now a large black dog. It was Little Bear, and he was licking Lucas.

As Lucas reached out to pet his friend, a series of sharp, stabbing pains shot up his legs. He thought they were on fire, but when he looked down, he saw that they were covered with blood.

As the pain lanced through him, the vision faded and was replaced by the stagecoach and passengers, which solidified and returned to their normal state. But the images remained bright in his mind, more clear than a memory, more real than a dream. It was his own father that Lucas had seen, and he was lying somewhere in the snow, dying.

Lucas bolted upright on the seat and threw off his blanket. Hadn't the others seen? he wondered. But everyone remained asleep, as if nothing had happened and no one was dying.

Lucas remembered Josiah's smile as he died . . . and he remembered Laurel's tears. The memory brought a sickening dread as he realized he might lose his own father, just as his mother had once been taken from him.

Lifting the blanket and wrapping it around his shoulders, Lucas stood and moved across to the door at Laurel's feet. He carefully turned the knob and pushed it open slightly. With a final glance at the sleeping passengers, he slipped outside, closed the door, and was gone into the night.

Several miles to the south, Quint Burgess regained consciousness. Beside him, Little Bear was curled up in the snow, licking Quint's face.

Quint's upper body was shivering uncontrollably with the cold, but his lower half was immobile and felt as if it were immersed in warm oil. As he reached over to Little Bear, a flood of pain coursed through his legs, and the warm oil started to boil. He clutched his chest as a wave of nausea surged through him and slowly passed. Tilting his head, he saw that his trousers were stiff with frozen blood, which fused the material to his skin. His legs felt as if they were caught in a red-hot vise, with any movement torturously tightening the grip.

Quint struggled to a sitting position, fighting the nausea and pain. His first thought was to make some sort of tourniquet, but he quickly realized that the bitter cold had already effectively stopped the bleeding.

Beside him, Little Bear stood up on shaky legs, his fur matted with blood. When the dog tried to lick his master's mangled legs, Quint had to push him away, but then he wrapped his arms around the animal and stammered, "It's—it's all r-r-right, Little Bear. Everything's all r-right."

The wind had died down, and the snowfall had lessened considerably. But it was still bitterly cold, and Quint realized he must find some sort of shelter if he was to survive the night. He also knew he did not have the strength to crawl more than a few feet.

Nearby, Quint saw the barrel of his shotgun protruding from the snow. Clenching his teeth, he rolled over onto his stomach. For a second, his vision clouded as the ground seemed to heave up and roll over him. But then the world steadied and his sight cleared. Marshaling all his strength, he began to drag himself through the snow, Little Bear following alongside.

At last reaching the shotgun, Quint leaned forward and grabbed the barrel, drawing the gun out of the snowdrift. With numbed fingers, he pulled it to him, leaning on it as he forced himself to sit back up. Clutching the frigid metal of the barrel in both hands, he stabbed the butt of the gun into the snow beside him and began to dig.

The storm was almost past. The wind had calmed, and the clouds were breaking up, allowing the full moon to slip in and out of view. Giant crystals of snow floated so slowly through the air that they seemed suspended on gossamer threads that swayed hypnotically in the delicate breeze. Even the temperature was beginning to rise as warm currents of air pushed like fingers from the south. Yet it was still well below freezing, and Arvis and Sadie Goode were too preoccupied with survival—and too hopelessly lost—to be aware of the changing weather.

Arvis hung on to the lead stage horse's collar with bare, frozen fingers. He had lost all feeling in his hands—had even lost awareness that he had hands—and he was thankful for it. Anything was an improvement over the agony he had experienced earlier when trying to protect his hands from the bitter wind while having to clutch onto bridle leather that was as cold and hard as a marble gravestone in winter.

The pain had shifted from Arvis's outer extremities to his chest, which felt like it was being squeezed by enormous ice tongs. With each gasp of breath, a frigid current invaded his lungs, until they were as fragile and brittle as a frozen rose. His uncovered head floated above the pain, disembodied and curiously hot, as if it were being consumed by a strange, infernal fire.

Through a glazed film, Arvis glanced back and saw a horse and rider behind him. He knew that person, but was having trouble remembering from where. She was completely covered by a thick woolen blanket, so that she appeared to be a monstrous headless horseman.

Arvis heard his voice crying, *"Sadie!"* and felt his lips fashioning the word, though he no longer remembered what it referred to. It was an instinctive cry, and it flowed from him again and again. It had some effect on the phantom behind him, however. The ghostly rider sat up in the saddle and stared at Arvis, its face hidden in shadows, revealing only the eyes, which were curiously devoid of life. Then the apparition looked down and continued to approach, as if prodding Arvis forward.

Overhead, leaning precariously against a neighboring tree, was an enormous, lightning-split limb—a widow-maker. Riding below, Arvis spun around in the saddle and shouted, *"Sadie!"* a final time. As the cry escaped his throat, an echoing wind shuddered through the trees. The limb twisted and slipped, suddenly hurtling down through the lower branches, snapping them like twigs.

The last thing Arvis was aware of before he was knocked off the horse into the black void was the image of that phantom rider looking up at him and the sound of her chilling, unearthly shriek.

Laurel Fox awoke with a start and immediately sensed that something was wrong. Around her, the other passengers were soundly sleeping, and for a moment she lay in the nearly pitch blackness and listened to their regular breathing. As her eyes began to focus in the darkness, she sat up on the center bench and looked about her. She saw the empty bench beside Tom Kennedy and at once knew where Lucas Burgess had gone.

Groping in her coat pocket, Laurel produced a match, which she struck and held to the lamp hanging overhead.

"Wh-what's going on?" the sleepy voice of Stephen Davis asked as he sat up straight, awakening his wife.

"Lucas has left," Laurel said. She pulled aside the leather window shade on the door and looked outside. It had stopped snowing, and from the height of the moon, she could tell that it was still several hours before dawn.

Tom Kennedy and Rebecca Williman woke up now, and Laurel turned to them and said, "Lucas isn't here. I think he went looking for Quint."

"Oh, my God, no," Merrilee murmured.

"Out there?" Rebecca said. "In the storm? He couldn't have. He'd freeze to death."

"Maybe he just had to relieve himself," Kennedy suggested.

"No. He is gone," Laurel said with conviction, not trying to explain her inner certainty.

"Then we'll have to go after him," Kennedy continued. Turning to Stephen, he asked, "Will you join me?"

"Me?" the young man said incredulously. "Out there? You're kidding. It was crazy of that driver to go in the first place, and now you want to compound it by getting us all killed?"

"Nobody's gonna die," Kennedy replied. "At least not if we find Lucas."

"What for?" Stephen asked. "He's just an idiot boy."

Laurel spun swiftly around, leaned across the aisle, and laid a stinging slap across the southerner's face. Stunned, Stephen grabbed his cheek. His eyes locked with Laurel's, and he appeared ready to strike back, but Merrilee placed a straining hand on his arm. The tense moment was broken as Laurel turned away and faced Tom Kennedy in the opposite corner.

"Yes. Lucas must be found," she agreed, "but not by you. I will go after him and bring him back."

"But you can't. You're a . . ." Kennedy's voice trailed off.

"Were you going to say 'woman'?" Laurel asked. "Why not Indian, because I am also that. And because of that, I know this land and how to survive in it."

Rebecca leaned forward and gave Laurel a gentle smile. "I think you've already proven you know how to survive better than any of us—woman or man. If you say you can find the boy, I'm sure you can."

Laurel nodded appreciatively at Rebecca.

"At least let me go with you," Kennedy offered.

"I'm sorry to be blunt, Tom, but you would only slow me down," Laurel replied. "No . . . this is something best handled on my own."

"But you're not dressed for such weather," Merrilee said in concern, looking at Laurel's coarse wool cloak and green velvet dress.

"I have a more suitable outfit in the back," Laurel assured her. "Just a minute while I get it."

Pulling up her fur-trimmed hood, Laurel opened the stagecoach door and stepped outside. For several minutes she searched the area around the coach, but the heavy snowfall and wind had obliterated any tracks.

Heading to the back of the coach, Laurel unstrapped the leather covering over the rear boot and yanked it aside. On the bottom of the boot to one side was a closed wooden compartment in which supplies were kept. She opened the front panel and rummaged inside, quickly producing a knife, hatchet, and rope, as well as a spare lantern. Laying the items on the front edge of the boot, she reached up and found a canvas knapsack of her father's. She dumped out the contents and refilled it with the supplies she had gathered.

Next Laurel removed her carpetbag from the pile of luggage and opened it on the edge of the boot. Folded inside were her long-legged winter britches and buckskin top. She untied and pulled off her cloak, laying it in the boot beside the carpetbag. Then she unbuttoned her shirt-waist dress and removed that, as well. Finally, she braced herself against the cold and stepped out of her underclothing. The awkward, high-laced shoes came off next, one by one. As each was removed, she slipped that leg into the leather britches and quickly put on one of the fur-lined moccasin boots that were at the bottom of the carpetbag. When both feet were covered, she pulled the britches all the way on, donned the heavy buckskin top, and laced the boots up around her calves.

Hoisting the knapsack over her shoulder and grabbing hold of the lantern, Laurel gathered up her cloak and returned to the coach. As she stepped back inside, the other passengers stared in wonder at this new woman who appeared before them. She looked radiantly beautiful in her intricately beaded outfit—and far more at ease than she had in her eastern-style clothing. No one spoke as she dropped the knapsack onto the center bench and lit the lantern, placing it beside the knapsack. Then she donned her cloak and strapped the knapsack onto her back.

"I've taken some supplies from the back of the coach," she announced as she picked up the lantern and backed through the doorway. "I will be as quick as I can—but don't worry if I don't return right away. There are no tracks in the snow, so Lucas must have left quite some time ago. If he has gone far and is suffering from exposure, it may be better to take him on to the way station where Quint was heading. In any case, just stay here until some-one comes for you. The sky is clear now, and I think the day will be warm. Nothing will happen to you as long as you stay put."

Laurel began to shut the door, but was stopped by Stephen Davis, who blocked it with his hand and stammered, "M-Miss Fox . . . I . . . I want you to know that we're praying for you. All of us."

Laurel smiled warmly at him. "Thank you, Stephen. Take care of the others." Then she closed the door and started south along the snow-covered stage road.

Sadie Goode sat leaning against a towering spruce tree in the open burrow she had carved in the snow. Her semiconscious husband lay sprawled on his back between her legs, his arms limp at his sides, his head cushioned against her chest. Sadie's large wool blanket covered them both.

Arvis's eyes rhythmically half opened and closed as Sadie slowly rocked him in her arms and hummed a lullaby. His thin, blue lips quivered with the trace of a smile as he felt the vibration of her voice. Magically, her coarse, brash tones filtered through to him as soft and sweet as when they were young and had just met. In his stupor, he thrilled at the memory of her full, saucy figure— before it had burst at the seams—and the fun-loving light that set fire to her eyes. He felt as if he had been nothing before finding Sadie—and what little he now was, she had made him. For Arvis, it was enough.

Arvis, however, was never enough for Sadie—or so she had always believed. She knew that he was gentle, considerate, and slavishly devoted to her, but like her own father, he was so damned clumsy and ineffectual. And as she stared down at him and felt his labored breathing, she realized that he was well on his way to bungling yet another caper—one that virtually had been held out for the taking.

"Don't mess up on me, Arvis," she muttered under her breath. "Dammit, don't do this to me."

Arvis opened his eyes fully and looked up at his wife.

In a faint, faltering voice, he whispered, "The money . . . you get the money?"

Sadie stared curiously at Arvis, then replied, "Uh, sure, I've got it right here in the saddlebag." She patted the bag, which lay in the snow at her side.

"Good," he breathed in relief. "And old man Grady wasn't the wiser."

"Grady?" Sadie asked, then remembered the shopkeeper they had swindled. "But, Arvis, that was in Farmington."

Arvis's eyes closed, and his smile broadened. "See, dear? I didn't botch things up this time. While you distracted him, I took the money. Didn't I?"

Sadie was about to remind him that he had immediately proceeded to drop the money on the floor, but something in his expression stopped her. Instead, she murmured, "Yes, Arvis, you took the money."

Arvis sighed. "Then we better catch the stage. There are many more sheep to be sheared."

"We already caught the stage, Arvis," she tried to remind him. "Don't you remember? We took all their money and the horses. We were heading to Durango, but you insisted on turning back. I don't know why I followed you, but you sure as hell couldn't survive on your own. Never could, damned fool." The tone of her final words was almost endearing—for Sadie.

Opening his eyes, Arvis tilted his head, as if listening to some inner voice. "It's cold, I think," he said.

"Damned fool," Sadie repeated as she reached forward and took both his hands in hers. Feeling how cold they were, she clasped the palms together in a gesture of prayer and began to rub them between her hands. "It'll be all right," she soothed. "I'll take care of you."

Arvis looked back up at Sadie, his eyes imploring as he asked, "Hold my hands, dear . . . won't you hold my hands? It's so cold."

Sadie stared at him a long moment, then looked at his frostbitten fingers. Her expression suddenly darkened, and as she dropped his hands, she blurted, "Don't do this to me, Arvis! Don't leave me! It's not fair!"

". . . So cold," he repeated, his eyelids lowering.

"I came back with you, didn't I? I agreed to return those damned horses to that accursed coach. And I'll do it—I promise. Just don't leave me!"

Arvis's breathing grew more shallow, as did his smile.

"Damn you!" she abruptly shouted, shaking his shoulders. "You won't do this, I say! What the hell will I do with all that money? Where will I go?"

The jostling roused him slightly, and he looked up and asked, "Are we there yet, my love? Got to get the horses back. It's so cold, and that old man is so sick."

"We'll get the horses back," she promised. "Just hang on. If you just hang on, I'll even give them back what we stole. The money, the jewelry—everything. What the hell am I going to do with it, anyway?"

". . . So cold . . . so tired . . ." His eyes began to roll up, the lids closing. Suddenly Arvis forced them open and, with a look of fear, asked, "You do love me, don't you?" His eyes sought hers, but seemed to look right through her. Slowly his expression sagged, and his eyes once again closed.

Sadie shook him fiercely, determined to stir up what life remained in him. But Arvis's only response was a sharp inhalation, followed by the soft whisper of air seeping through his lips. He breathed no more.

Sadie felt his body go limp, but it did not register in her mind. Her eyes lost their focus for a second, and her head began to loll to the side. Then her entire body jerked, and she seemed to shake off her stupor. She glanced back at her husband, and with one hand, she reached longingly toward his cheek, pulling away just before she touched the skin.

Sadie's eyes opened wide. "Arvis?" Then she squinted, her brow wrinkling. "What do you want of me?" she asked in the faintest of voices. "To say that I love you? I—I love you . . ." Her voice trailed off, and even she did not know whether she had answered or merely repeated the question.

Sadie sat for long minutes, rocking Arvis in her arms and humming a lullaby. Magically, she heard her husband's delicate voice accompanying her, sweetening her own coarse tones.

In the distance, one of the stage horses stamped restlessly. The four animals were still tied together, with Ned Purvis's saddle horse nuzzling the snow nearby.

As the storm subsided and the moon appeared from behind a cloudbank, Sadie glanced up and saw the animals. Gently cradling Arvis's head in her arms, she lifted it off her lap, lowered him to the ground beside her, and rose to her knees. She undraped the blanket from around her shoulders and tenderly covered him with it. Sadie was no longer humming, though in her mind the music played on.

"Yes, you do look tired," she told him, picking up his earlier remark as if it had just been uttered. "And indeed, you must rest."

She cocked her head, as if listening, then continued, "Yes, of course you are right. What need have we of earthly treasures, when we have each other? I'll be but a minute, and after I return the horses and money, you will be strong enough to go on."

Sadie smiled at her husband, then leaned forward and kissed him lovingly on the forehead. She began to reach for the saddlebag beside her, but suddenly turned back and threw her arms around Arvis's neck. Her lips fused passionately with his as she clutched him to her. Finally she relaxed the embrace and eased his head back against the snow. She stood slowly to her feet, lifted the saddlebag over her shoulder, and wandered off toward the horses.

The stage team looked up as the big woman approached. She was stumbling erratically through the snow, one hand clutching a saddlebag, the other reaching toward them. The lead horse snorted, flicked its tail, and walked a few feet farther away, the other horses trailing behind. But the woman kept coming, her arm groping wildly through the air. As the lead horse reared up slightly, the others whinnied with fear.

Twenty feet away, the saddle horse watched disinterestedly as the string of stage horses broke into a gallop and disappeared into the dark forest. The woman did not seem to notice him, but kept on walking forward, so the saddle horse went back to nuzzling in the snow at the grass below.

Sadie Goode wandered into the night, the horses all but forgotten now. What guided her was her promise to Arvis, who was resting so patiently as he awaited her return. His memory would be more than sufficient to sustain her and see her through.

As Arvis Goode's body, laid out in the snow, gave up the last of its warmth, his wife's moist kiss slowly crystallized upon his lips.

Chapter Nine

The moon had set, but the sky continued to soften as dawn approached. For more than a mile, there had been no tracks in the snow for Laurel Fox to follow. But then she had come upon a trampled area among some large boulders beside the road, where Lucas Burgess apparently had taken refuge at some point during his journey. Undoubtedly the weather that had forced him to seek shelter had also obliterated the tracks he had made coming from the stagecoach. Lucas must have waited there for the storm to lessen, because south of the boulders, his small footprints were clear and easy to follow.

Fifteen minutes later, Laurel caught sight of the boy in the distance. He was plowing awkwardly through the drifts, wrapped in one of the huge stagecoach blankets.

"Lucas!" she called. *"Lucas!"*

He did not respond, so Laurel went racing up the hill, shouting his name, her long, open cloak streaming behind.

As Lucas stumbled through the snow, impelled by the force of his inner vision, he was barely aware of his surroundings. All he knew was that he had to reach his father—that somehow everything would be all right if he reached Quint in time. Suddenly he sensed rather than heard something approaching, and he spun around a moment before it caught up to him.

He caught a glimpse of moccasins and beaded leather, of arms reaching out and grabbing his shoulders. In his trancelike state, Lucas could not focus clearly, but in a shock of awareness, it registered that he was being attacked—by Indians! His body went rigid with fear as he squeezed shut his eyes and waited for death to strike.

"Don't be afraid," a voice said. "It's Laurel. I've come to help you." But the words were a meaningless jumble as the constant background of noise inside Lucas's head began to explode with hysteria.

Trying to squelch the clamor, Lucas shook his head wildly. He struggled to pull away from his attacker, but the huge Indian clutched his arms all the more tightly.

"Lucas, you must come back to the stagecoach with me. Your father—"

With a sudden yank, Lucas slipped from beneath the blanket and pulled free. He spun around and raced up the road.

"Lucas!"

The boy thought he heard his name being shouted, but he ran blindly forward, sensing that the Indian was in pursuit.

Powerful arms reached out and grabbed him around the chest, pulling him close. Lucas became frantic, swinging and striking out with his arms and legs, but the Indian lifted him off his feet, and he found himself kicking the air. As he opened his lips and mouthed a silent scream, the Indian slipped one hand up and grasped his head, pulling it backward until his cheek was pressed against the beads on the chest of the leather shirt.

"Lucas, easy now," Laurel soothed, her words lost in his continued frenzy. She hugged him tightly to her and began to hum a deep-throated chant.

Lucas felt as if he were trapped by a huge, smothering animal, his brain being pounded by great clashing peals of thunder. Nothing made sense in this cacophony of noise, except his compulsion to escape and reach his father. Then he noticed that the noise had taken on a deep, rhythmic drone, which at first frightened him further. But as the drone increased in intensity, sliding effortlessly up and down the register of sound, it began to diffuse the other, more strident tones.

Lucas's body slowly relaxed as he felt the vibrations passing through his cheek and chest and filling him with an ineffable calm. It was music he was hearing, he now realized, and it came not from an Indian warrior, but from the voice of a woman. Hesitantly, Lucas opened his eyes and looked up into Laurel's smile.

"Lucas," she whispered, kissing his forehead. She kneeled down with him in the snow, holding the young boy in her lap.

They sat together for a long moment, Laurel humming a gentle Ute song, Lucas with his head against her chest, remembering the sweetness of his mother's lullaby. But then he pulled back slightly and looked at her, his eyes tense and his lips quivering with worry.

"What is it, Lucas?" she slowly asked, carefully mouthing each word.

The boy shook his head slightly, as if indicating he did not understand her question.

Laurel lifted Lucas to his feet and kneeled in front of him, so that their eyes were level. Using the simplest of signs, she pointed at him and at herself, then gestured that they must return down the trail to the stagecoach.

Lucas's eyes opened wider, and he shook his head furiously. When she tried to repeat the sign, he let her get as far as indicating the two of them. But when she tried to gesture toward the stage, he turned her hand so that she was pointing in the direction Quint had gone.

Laurel smiled as she said, "No, we must go to the stagecoach."

Again Lucas shook his head and pointed to the south. His lips puckered, as if he was struggling to speak.

Realizing the name the boy was trying to fashion, Laurel said, "Quint?" When he immediately nodded his head, Laurel asked, "What about Quint?"

Lucas's only response was to continue mouthing his father's name, while pointing up the trail.

"Quint is fine," Laurel tried to assure him. "He went to get horses. He will be back soon."

Lucas shook his head, while mouthing "Quint" and waving wildly to the south.

"We must get back," Laurel insisted.

As she reached out and gently took his arm, she felt his body go rigid. He clamped shut his eyes and abruptly let out a piercing, piteous wail. Laurel quickly let go of him and clasped her hands together. His scream subsided, and he looked back at her with pleading, mournful eyes. Then he raised his arms to her, opened his mouth, and stammered, "Qu-Qu-Qui . . . Quint!"

Laurel opened her arms, and the young boy rushed into them. She held him close and stroked his hair as he sobbed and repeated, "Quint, Quint, Quint, Quint, Quint . . ."

As Lucas began to calm, Laurel whispered, "You spoke . . . his name . . . you spoke," her eyes clouding with tears.

The boy pulled back and looked longingly into her eyes as he said, "Qu-Quint . . ."

"What is it?" Laurel asked, gripping his shoulders. "What about Quint?"

Lucas moved his lips as if searching for words, then bowed his head in frustration and began to cry.

"It's all right," Laurel assured him, lifting his chin so that he was again looking at her. "Don't talk. Speak with your hands." She raised his hands in her own. "Use your hands."

Lucas's eyes brightened, and he slipped his hands from hers and stepped back a few feet. First he pointed up the trail in the direction Quint had gone. Then he pointed down at the snow. When Laurel shook her head to indicate she did not understand, he walked down the trail and picked up the blanket that had fallen when he had run away from her. He carried it back to where Laurel was still kneeling, wrapped it around himself, and lay down in the snow, curling up like a ball and staring at her with wide eyes.

Laurel waited, but the boy did not move. "Lucas," she called, standing and slowly approaching him. "Lucas?"

Still he did not stir, and Laurel stooped down and nudged his shoulder. "What is it? Is something wrong with you?"

Lucas immediately nodded his head and sat up. Again he nodded and pointed up the road.

"Quint? Something is wrong with Quint?" she asked.

Lucas nodded briskly and mouthed, "Yes."

"How do you know?" Laurel asked, but the boy merely looked at her as if pleading to be understood.

As Laurel stared into his eyes, she suddenly thought of the Ute medicine man Surnia . . . her grandfather. He had spoken so often with his eyes. Indeed, much of his knowledge had been taught not by what he said, but by what was left unsaid. Surnia had always valued the inner voice above all music, and he had taught her to trust the language of the heart.

A tear rolled down Lucas's cheek. As Laurel wiped it away, the thought struck her that a child such as this— someone lost in a world without verbal communication— must be aware of songs rarely perceived by those who listen with their ears. And while there had been no Surnia in Lucas's life, the truest teacher was the inner voice itself—and throughout his life, this child had been its apprentice.

Laurel delicately took the boy's face in her hands and closed her eyes. She breathed deeply and concentrated on the energy that she could feel coursing to her through her arms. She tried to relax her body as she listened for a voice and waited for her inner eye to open.

It might have been merely a random image in her mind, but Laurel could see Quint lying unconscious in the snow, Little Bear whimpering beside him. And somehow she knew it was the very vision that had been Lucas's guide.

Opening her eyes, Laurel caressed his face and smiled. "Let us find Quint," she said, pointing to the south. Taking hold of Lucas's hand, she led the way up the road in the thin, predawn light.

After Laurel left the stagecoach, the other passengers were too wide awake to consider going back to sleep. Instead, as the night creeped toward dawn, they sat up talking, Stephen and Merrilee holding each other on the forward bench, while Rebecca sat beside Tom Kennedy on the rear bench.

Perhaps it was the long night or the early hour or the exhausting ride, but the passengers felt suspended in a place without time, as if nothing existed beyond the interior of the coach. And though they were stranded in the middle of a freak autumn blizzard, they felt unusually warm and secure.

Stephen Davis was the quietest of the group—a fact particularly noted by Rebecca. At one point when he seemed overly pensive, she leaned forward and said, "Thank you, Stephen, for telling Laurel we would be praying for her. It expressed my sentiments precisely."

Merrilee smiled up at her husband. "I was proud when you said that to Laurel," she whispered.

Stephen's return smile held a note of embarrassment. "But not so proud when I called Lucas an idiot boy, I'll wager," he replied.

"I understand."

"Well, I don't," Stephen said grimly. "That boy never did anything to annoy me. I had no call."

"Sometimes we don't need any reason," Kennedy put in. "Hell, I've said far worse. It's like I have all this anger at myself, and I end up taking it out on whoever is nearest. At the time, it seems a hell of a lot easier than taking it out on me."

"I get that way when I feel insecure," Rebecca offered. "That's when I tend to do foolish things."

"But sometimes foolish things turn out right," Merrilee noted. "Like when I married Stephen."

"That was foolish?" her husband asked with a mock frown.

Merrilee blushed. "I didn't mean it to sound like that, but in a way it was. You know how insecure I felt at home. My father is so talented, and my mother is . . . well, perfect. I always felt unworthy . . . insignificant."

"But everyone is in love with you. You are always the gayest, the most beautiful . . ."

Seeing Merrilee's uncomfortable expression, Rebecca said, "Beauty, Stephen, can sometimes be a great burden. Your wife's extraordinary beauty may have made her feel that people gave their love not to her, but to her image."

Seeing that his wife was nodding in agreement, Stephen said, "Is that why you thought marrying me was foolish? Do you think I married you for your beauty?"

"Oh, no, Stephen, not at all," Merrilee vowed. "Just the opposite. You were the only one who valued my opinions and my company."

"Then what was so foolish?" he pressed.

"I probably shouldn't have used that word. What I meant was that I may have married you for many of the wrong reasons. I was looking for someone to give me the security I couldn't find in myself.''

Stephen hesitated, then slowly said, ''You didn't love me?''

''Oh, my dearest, of course I loved you—I *do* love you. But I haven't always been fair to you. I wanted you to be strong for both of us, and so I failed you.''

Stephen pulled her head to his shoulder. ''You've never failed me. And I *can* be strong enough for us both.''

Merrilee sat up abruptly. ''No! Please don't do that. When you try to be strong—your father's kind of strong—it's almost as if I don't recognize you. You showed far more strength when you spoke so kindly to Laurel.''

Stephen chuckled. ''My father certainly wouldn't have done that.''

''It sounds like your father has a lot to learn about true courage,'' Kennedy suggested.

''I can't say about that,'' Stephen answered, ''but I do know that imitating him never seems to work. Damned if I haven't tried just about everything to please him—to be like him. It just doesn't fit on me. I suppose I have some kind of demon inside of me that won't be satisfied until . . . until . . .'' His words trailed off in thought.

''I can tell you something about that demon,'' Rebecca spoke up. ''I know it, because I've faced it with my father. I can also tell you that what you've been looking for is your father's blessing.''

''I think that's exactly it,'' Stephen admitted.

''I'm afraid you'll never get it by trying to please him,'' Rebecca said.

''Yes, I know that now,'' Stephen replied somewhat dejectedly. ''I think I realized it when Josiah Fox was saying good-bye to Laurel. It was as if she had been doing everything he wanted just to please him. But in the end he realized that what she did was worthwhile only if it came from her own heart. If by living a lie I succeed in receiving my own father's blessing, it is as meaningless as if it had been given to someone else. I suppose it's about time I began living my own life, regardless of what Frederick Davis thinks or says.'' Stephen smiled at his wife, and she affectionately squeezed his hand.

''I wish I had learned that lesson while my father was alive,'' Rebecca mused. ''I've told you how similar our fathers were. I don't think Hughes ever got over his bitter disappointment that I was born a female. All his life he withheld his love, and he never gave any kind of blessing before he died. It's true that I hated him—almost as much as I loved him.''

''And he deserved to be hated,'' Kennedy pointed out. ''I know the way he used to beat you.'' Seeing Rebecca wince, he continued, ''You never had the chance to please him. Nobody did. His self-professed code of behavior was totally arbitrary and was changed at his slightest whim. And when he thought someone broke that code, he made them pay.''

''That may be true, but it still hurt when he rejected my love.''

Across the aisle, Merrilee sighed and nodded. ''I think there would be nothing worse than not feeling loved by your parents,'' she said.

''Yes,'' Rebecca agreed, ''but I think what hurts the most—and the deepest—is the knowledge that perhaps I could have tried harder to save Hughes when our house burned down. Instead, I just stood there and didn't do a thing. Why? Was it out of hate?''

''Perhaps you merely were afraid that if you tried, you might fail him again,'' Merrilee suggested.

Suddenly Rebecca's eyes misted with tears. As she leaned forward and began to sob, Tom Kennedy moved closer and put his arm around her.

''It's all right,'' Kennedy soothed. ''You weren't the only one to hate Hughes Williman, and you weren't the only one to be relieved when he died." Rebecca stopped crying, but sat with her eyes closed, her head leaning on his shoulder.

Kennedy looked up at the Davises and continued, "It was seven years ago that I asked Hughes Williman's permission to marry Abigail, the family cook. He refused, claiming that marriage would interfere with our duties. Now, I certainly could have gone ahead and married her—the Civil War was long over. But I caved in to his threat to fire us both if we didn't obey him."

"That must have been so painful," Merrilee said.

"It was, and it got worse. Two months later I discovered the real reason he was standing in our way. You see, he had been sharing Abigail's bed for quite some time, and he didn't want to lose his 'privileges.' God, how angry I was—mostly at Abigail. I knew he had coerced her, yet I could never find it in myself to forgive her. So I began bedding her myself and never again offered to marry her."

Rebecca leaned up and touched Kennedy's cheek. "I'm so sorry," she said. "I knew what was going on, but I was too weak to stand up for you."

Kennedy stared off into the distance. "I hated him so much. That was why I didn't want to save him in that fire."

Rebecca sat up and looked at him. "But you know that isn't true." She turned to the Davises. "He was the only one who tried to do anything. He ran into that blazing building and tried to pull my father out."

"It wasn't really like that," Kennedy said. "I waited a long time, praying your father was slowly burning in Hell. Then I realized that, by not acting, I would end up hating myself—and that Hughes would be the winner, even in death. So I ran in there, hoping he already was dead. And he was."

"It wasn't your fault," Rebecca said.

"You don't understand," Kennedy continued. "It

wasn't the fire that killed him. He was dead already. He had shot himself in the head.''

"My God," Rebecca murmured and began to sob.

Kennedy held her close and whispered, "I'm sorry, Rebecca. I'm so sorry."

There was a long silence. As Rebecca began to calm, Stephen commented, "It's understandable. A bullet might well have seemed preferable to fire."

"No, it wasn't the fire," Kennedy said. He turned to Rebecca. "There's more, if you want to hear it." He waited until she slowly nodded, then continued, "Your father set that fire. Then he shot himself. I think he burned down the mansion because he wanted to take everyone with him. He always claimed none of us could live without him."

"B-but how?" Rebecca stammered. "How d-do you know?"

"There was a suicide note, but it rambled and didn't make any sense. I decided to leave him in the study and let the fire take him. I thought it would be less painful for you if everyone thought it was an accident. Later, I even burned the note."

As Rebecca looked into his eyes and saw that he was telling the truth, she again began to cry.

"I'm sorry. I should have told you before. I didn't know you were blaming yourself for his death. I should have known that hiding the truth doesn't change it."

Rebecca's sobbing slowly faded, until they sat in silence. Kennedy continued to hold Rebecca, rocking her gently in his arms. Across the coach, Stephen held his wife closer, and she leaned up and caressed his cheek.

Their solitude was broken by a feeble rapping against the stagecoach door.

"Laurel," Merrilee whispered as her husband quickly stood and opened the door.

Outside, an apparition covered in ice pushed into the

doorway. A wild gleam lit her eyes as Sadie Goode muttered, "See, dear, I've made it! I did it for you! Now you don't have to worry. They will forgive us, and you can sleep peacefully in the snow."

Sadie Goode fell forward, and the saddlebag dropped from her shoulder, spilling the passengers' valuables across the floor of the coach.

Kennedy leaped up and helped Stephen hoist Sadie through the door and up onto the center bench. She lay there, her eyes wide, her face frozen into a smile. "Forgive us . . . now they will forgive us . . ." she whispered as the heaving of her chest subsided.

"Yes, yes, we forgive you," Merrilee blurted out as she frantically took the woman's hands and began to rub.

It was the last thing Sadie Goode heard. With her eyes fixed on the lamplight overhead, she took their forgiveness and carried it back to her husband's waiting arms.

The temperature rose dramatically as the sun lifted into a clear sky and warm air continued to push toward the Rockies from the desert to the southeast. Laurel removed her hood and looked up through the trees, gauging the day ahead. It would feel like a return to summer—Indian summer, as the whites called it—and in a few hours the snow cover would be but a memory.

Laurel wrapped her arm around Lucas Burgess's shoulder, and the boy looked up and smiled at her. Yet she could read the worry that continued to etch his face as they headed toward the way station without having found any trace of his father.

"We will be with Quint soon," she assured Lucas, hugging him to her. Lucas lifted her arm from his shoulder and pulled it around to stroke his cheek.

Just then a thin yelp cut the stillness. Laurel heard it and pulled Lucas to a halt. She stood listening for a minute, and at the same moment that she heard the yelping again, they both saw a black animal come limping toward them through the snow.

"Little Bear!" Laurel shouted.

Lucas was already pointing at his dog, and then he broke from Laurel and ran to the animal. As he dropped to his knees and threw his arms around Little Bear's neck, the dog's soft yelp turned into a sharp cry of pain.

"He's hurt!" Laurel cried as she raced over to them.

Lucas realized what was wrong, and he moved aside and gently patted Little Bear's back while Laurel quickly examined him.

"He's been in a fight," she told Lucas. "A fight," she repeated, and Lucas nodded that he understood.

"I don't think the wounds are too extensive," she continued as she gently ran her fingers through the dog's fur, "but Little Bear has lost blood and is weak. There is only one deep gash that is still bleeding. It must be sutured at once."

Laurel looked over at Lucas and realized he had no idea what she was talking about. With her hands, she imitated the act of sewing a wound and then pointed at the cut below Little Bear's right front shoulder. Lucas immediately nodded, then placed his head on the dog's back and hugged.

Laurel reached into the pocket of her cloak and pulled out a small leather bag. She untied the drawstring and searched through the contents. Among the tweezers, pocket knife, and rolls of gauze were a needle and ligature threads. Choosing one of the ligatures, she deftly threaded the needle, then closed up the bag and returned it to her pocket.

"Hold him steady," she carefully pronounced, smiling as Lucas complied.

Little Bear's faith in his master was so complete that he barely moved as Laurel pierced his skin and closed the wound. He gave only one small whimper when she tied it off and cut the thread. Then, as if understanding that he had been helped, Little Bear began to wag his tail and prance in place. It was as if the act of stitching that single wound had miraculously healed all the dog's pain.

Laurel lifted the dog's face to hers and asked, "Where is Quint? Quint! Take us to Quint!"

Little Bear began to bark. He pulled away from Laurel and Lucas and started up the trail, then turned around and looked back at them.

"Yes, Little Bear, find Quint!" Laurel repeated, and Lucas nodded and pointed up the trail. Little Bear spun around and raced up the road, pausing every few moments to make certain they were following.

Five minutes later, Laurel saw a tiny patch of fur atop a mound of snow. She ran toward it, Lucas racing alongside. As they neared the mound, Laurel grabbed hold of Lucas and held him back, fearful of what they might discover. She tried to get him to stay where he was, but Lucas would not be left behind, so she put her arm around him as they cautiously approached.

The fur was at the top of a three-foot-high, circular wall of snow that seemed unusually solid and packed down. Near the base of one side there was a small tunnel, at which Little Bear now pawed and barked. Laurel leaned against the wall and peered over the top. She knew at once that the fur she had seen was a patch of Quint's bearskin coat, sticking up above the snow. She tugged at it with one hand while brushing off snow with the other.

Suddenly the fur shifted on its own, and they heard a moan. Digging furiously, Laurel and Lucas uncovered the rest of the coat and pulled it aside. Below, in a hollowed out snow cave, Quint lay curled up on his side. As the sunlight hit him, he feebly opened his eyes and smiled up at them.

Ten minutes later, the walls of snow had been demolished, and Quint lay on his back, telling of his ordeal. Laurel tried to keep him quiet, but Quint would not relax until he had fully recounted his run-in with the wild dogs and how he had passed out in the snow. He knew he would have died if Little Bear had not awakened him in the middle of the night. He then had dug this crude snow cave and taken shelter with Little Bear in the relative warmth inside. The small tunnel in the wall of snow apparently had been made when Little Bear had dug himself out earlier that morning to go in search of help.

Laurel carefully cut away the legs of Quint's pants and examined his injuries. Since the bleeding had stopped, she decided against further treating any of the wounds out here on the road. Instead she would bandage the legs and treat him back at the coach, where there were additional medical supplies.

Using cloth from the knapsack, she tightly wrapped his legs in pressure bandages. After they were secured, she used Lucas's blanket to wrap Quint's legs.

"You cannot walk," Laurel announced, and Quint nodded his head. "Do you know where we are?"

"I think about halfway between the stagecoach and the way station. You could leave me here and continue on to the sta—"

"No, I won't leave you," Laurel cut in, wondering whether her response came from sound medical judgment or an unwillingness to be away from Quint now that she had found him. "It's downhill to the coach, and that's where we will take you. I'll go for help after I treat your injuries."

"But how—?"

"Don't worry yourself about it, Quint. There are ways to get you there—Indian ways. You just rest here." With that she took Lucas by the arm and led him into the forest.

Under Laurel's guidance, Lucas helped gather short, sturdy branches, as well as two long poles that curved up at one end. Using rope from the knapsack, they tied the upturned ends of the poles together, spreading apart the other ends to form a long *V*. Then they placed the thinner branches crosswise on the poles and lashed them in place to form a small, makeshift sled, which they pulled back through the forest to where Quint was lying.

Laurel and Lucas helped Quint roll over onto the sled. When he was comfortably in place on his back, Laurel took another length of rope and tied the ends to the upturned point of the sled. Calling Little Bear over, she wrapped the looped end of the rope around the dog's shoulders and fashioned a harness.

Under Laurel's direction, Lucas took his place at the foot of the sled and prepared to push. Laurel, meanwhile, positioned herself beside the upturned point, where she could help pull. Little Bear looked back at them, eager to be put to the test.

At her command, he leaped forward in the harness, struggling against the inertia as Laurel and Lucas added their weight to the task. The sled jerked, momentarily halted, then began to slide forward through the snow. As Little Bear barked and bounded down the hill, the sled slowly picked up speed, until Laurel and Lucas no longer needed to push, but instead found themselves holding the contraption back.

"Whooee!" Quint shouted, winking up at his grinning son as the sled raced faster and faster through the snow.

Chapter Ten

Stephen Davis and Tom Kennedy had no difficulty following the tracks in the snow made by Sadie Goode. They had set off together shortly after Sadie died, hoping that Arvis might still be alive and that the stage horses could be found. Now as the sun rose and began to warm the chill air, they were following a wildly meandering trail through the woods.

"It is incredible that Sadie ever found the stagecoach," Stephen commented upon reaching one point where her tracks made a wide arc and then crossed over themselves.

"God knows how many hours she was wandering around out here," Kennedy put in. He looked down at the tracks and added with a smile, "You sure those are *her* footprints? The way you've been leading us around in circles, they just might be yours coming around again!"

With a gleam in his eyes, Stephen looked down at his feet, then over at Kennedy's. Finally, he pointed at the footprints in the snow and said, "No, I'm afraid those tracks couldn't have been made by me. Hell, look at the size of them! Only two folks around here I know of with feet that big. . . ." He paused, giving Kennedy a sheepish grin, then concluded, "Sadie Goode and you, Tom Kennedy!"

As Kennedy began to chuckle, the young southerner

suddenly put a finger to his lips and whispered, "Shhh! Look!" He pointed through the trees to where four horses stood huddled in a clearing, their bridles strung together.

"The stage team!" Kennedy whispered back. "Let's go get them!"

"Wait," Stephen said, grabbing Kennedy's sleeve to restrain him. "We can't just barge over there."

"Why not?"

"We don't want them to spook and run off," Stephen explained. "We're upwind, so we'd better circle around. I'll go to the left, you to the right. When we get opposite each other, I want you to start walking very calmly toward them. If you can get hold of one of the bridles, great. But if they spook, I'll be waiting on the other side."

"Sounds like you've done this sort of thing before," Kennedy commented. "You weren't kidding when you said you've been around horses."

"It's in my breeding," Stephen replied, chuckling as he added, "I told you I'm a Georgia thoroughbred."

"You just be careful over there," Kennedy urged. "If they come charging, don't get yourself killed."

"Isn't much chance of that—not if you approach them slowly. They'll probably just get a bit skittish and start backing away from you. They'll never even see me until I've got them. The risk is that they might get really scared and take off at a gallop, so go real slow. I don't want to have to stalk them all over Colorado."

"Then don't worry, because *my* breeding perfectly suits me to the task. I'll just pretend I'm with my ancestors stalking lions in Africa. One thing you never want to face is a skittish lion!" The two men laughed, then Kennedy turned and headed through the trees to the right.

Stephen watched for a moment, then began to circle to the left. A couple of minutes later he saw that they were both in position, so he raised his arm and waved Kennedy forward. As the black man started cautiously toward the horses, Stephen slipped carefully from tree to tree toward the clearing.

Despite Kennedy's caution, the horses caught sight of him approaching and became nervous. The lead horse raised its head and snorted, while the others began backing away. The lead horse then shook its mane and stamped its foot. As the black man continued to approach, the horse followed the others toward the trees behind them.

Stephen was hidden behind a tree at the edge of the clearing. When the back of one of the horses was only ten feet away, the young southerner slipped silently from behind the tree and raced across the clearing. By the time the horse took notice, Stephen was beside it and had reached up to grab the bridle.

The horse reared up, yanking the bridle from Stephen's grip. The other horses began to panic, and in the milling confusion, Stephen managed to grab the bridle again. Tom Kennedy was running toward them now, but before he could reach the horses, they went into a frenzy. At first the team pulled in all directions, then they fell into step and began to stampede in a wide circle around the clearing, Stephen hanging on to the last horse, fighting to stay on his feet.

Kennedy tried to grab onto one of the animals, but his action only served to increase their panic. The lead horse found a large gap between a few of the trees, and he wheeled the team in that direction. The last Kennedy saw of Stephen Davis as the horses raced from the clearing, he was being dragged through the snow, his hands caught in the leather of the rear horse's bridle.

Stephen fought to regain his footing, his legs bouncing along the ground as the horses barreled recklessly through the trees. His hands were hopelessly tangled in the leather, and he realized that he probably could not free them if he tried. He did not want to, anyway, since that would surely mean losing the horses. So he hung on, praying for an opportunity to bring the team under control.

Stephen's chance came when the team slowed to avoid a close cropping of trees. Gripping the bridle, the young man pulled himself forward, took a running leap, and vaulted onto the horse's back. He made it only halfway and found himself hanging sideways as the stage team rounded the trees and took off at a gallop.

Stephen felt his strength giving way as he struggled to right himself on the horse. His left hand slipped free of the bridle, and he almost toppled from the horse. But he managed to grab the animal's mane, and with a final exertion, he pulled himself onto the animal's back. He lay there on his stomach for a moment as he worked to free his right hand from the bridle leather. Then clutching the straps in both hands, he pulled himself to a sitting position and yanked back on the bridle.

The horse fought the bit and continued to race after its mates. Again and again Stephen yanked the horse's head back, but to no avail. It flew on, its head reared high as it blindly followed the rest of the team.

It was as the horses rounded a large pine that the overhanging branch suddenly appeared, head high. Stephen saw it too late. He dropped down and hugged the horse's back, pulling down on the bridle to lower the animal's head. But the horse reacted too slowly, and the branch smashed across the top of its head.

The animal stumbled and went down, the other horses tangling in the line and falling, as well.

Stephen rolled free and found himself lying against the trunk of a tree. He sat up, rubbed his head, and looked over at the animals. Two were already standing, and the third was struggling to its feet. The rear horse lay on its side, whimpering and flailing its legs.

Stephen stood cautiously, feeling to make sure he had not broken any bones. Then he hurried over to where the rear horse was lying.

"Easy, boy!" he urged as he patted the animal's neck.

The horse looked up at him and began to calm. When its legs had stopped kicking, Stephen carefully ran his hands along the animal's flanks and down each leg.

"It doesn't feel like you broke anything," he said. "Let's try to get you up."

Stephen patted the horse's head as he took hold of the bridle. "C'mon, boy," he said as he pulled the animal forward.

The horse at first resisted, then suddenly rolled sideways and tried to rise up. As it slipped back down into the snow, Stephen tugged again at the bridle.

"That's it, fella, you can do it!"

This time the horse rocked back and forth and stood precariously on its feet. Stephen immediately examined each of its legs, then came around to the front and patted its nose.

"You're fine, boy, just fine. Now, how about a walk?"

He eased the horse forward, watching closely as it took its first hesitant steps. Slowly the animal's confidence returned, and in a few moments he had it walking in circles, leading the rest of the horses behind.

"It's time we got on with business," Stephen said as he led the animals back through the trees.

They had not gone far before Tom Kennedy appeared in the distance, racing toward them.

"You all right?" Kennedy called as he came running up.

"Hell, that's the way we always mount a horse in Georgia!" Stephen exclaimed.

"No wonder you lost the war!" Kennedy said, slapping him on the back, and they both roared with laughter.

A half mile farther to the north, at the end of the trail

of footprints in the snow, the body of Arvis Goode lay frozen among the trees.

"At least he looks like he died peacefully," Stephen Davis said as he and Tom Kennedy stood over the body, the stage horses tied to a nearby tree.

"That's quite a bruise on the side of his head," Kennedy noted as he stooped down and touched Arvis's face. Standing back up, he looked around at the scattered debris in the snow and said, "See the way that big limb and all those branches landed on top of the snow—not buried under it? They must have fallen in the storm, and I'll bet that big one took Arvis with it."

Stephen scanned the trees above. "There are a hell of a lot of broken branches up there. We'd better get out of here before we end up beside him."

"I think we ought to bring his body back to the coach so he can be buried with his wife. Agreed?"

"Definitely," Stephen said. "Let's strap him to one of the horses."

With Kennedy at the shoulders and Stephen at the feet, the two men bent down and lifted Arvis's cold, stiff body. They carried it to the second horse in line and hoisted it face down over its back. As Kennedy secured it with leather straps from the harness, Stephen scouted the area, returning just as Kennedy was finishing his task.

"Find anything?" Kennedy asked. "Any sign of that horse Sadie was riding?"

"There are plenty of tracks. It looks like the horse wandered off to the northwest. Think it's worth going after?"

"How long might that take?"

"Could be hours," Stephen guessed.

"Then let's forget it. These four seem fit enough, and by the time we get back to the stage, Quint may have returned with four more."

"Let's get going then," Stephen agreed. He went

over to the tree and untied the line holding the horses. As he circled the animals toward the south, he said, "One of us ought to ride the lead horse, and the other the one right behind Arvis. It'd be better if no one rode that last one— give him more of a chance to recover from that fall."

"Sounds fine with me."

"Why don't you take the front spot, then?" Stephen offered.

"Hell, no, not me. I've seen you with horses, so this is your show." Kennedy paused as the two men looked at one another for a long moment. Then he added, "You know, you're going to make one damn fine horse breeder. You've got a firm but careful touch."

Stephen's expression darkened, and he stared down at the ground.

"Did I say something wrong?" Kennedy asked. "Is it that you don't want to raise horses—maybe because that's what your father expects of you? Just because he wants you to do something, you shouldn't automatically reject it. You've got to decide for yourself."

Stephen looked up and smiled. "It's more than that. I love horses, and I'd like to raise them—whether my father wants me to or not. I was just thinking of something that happened when I was younger."

"Want to talk about it?"

"Might as well. It won't change it, though."

Stephen began to lead the horses along the trail to the stagecoach, Tom Kennedy walking beside him.

"It happened nine years ago, in 1872," Stephen began. "I was twelve, and I had a best friend my age named . . . Willie."

Kennedy noted how difficult it was for Stephen to say his friend's name. "You don't have to talk about it."

"No, I'd like to. It's just that Willie . . . Willie was colored."

Kennedy grinned slightly. "Sort of hard figuring you

with a black friend. But that's natural for kids, and anyway it was well after the Civil War.''

"It wasn't natural in my family. My father put up with it for a time. I guess he figured it might give me some experience I could use as an adult. But . . . but our friendship ended pretty abruptly that year.''

Again Stephen fell into silence, and to ease the awkwardness, Kennedy picked up the conversation. "Well, I can see how you'd be carrying a lot of resentment against your father for breaking you and Willie apart. But you've got to remember he comes from another genera—''

"It wasn't my father," Stephen cut in. "It was me. I broke it apart.''

Stephen slipped his hand to his cheek and brushed away a tear. Kennedy turned so as not to notice.

"Don't be so hard on yourself," Kennedy finally said. "It's the way you were raised.''

"I suppose so, but there's more than that. Willie and I spent a lot of time together and often went bareback riding. We both loved horses—his father was our top groom. But then my father forbade me to associate with the servants, saying that at twelve I had to start assuming my proper role in life. I didn't listen, and I forced Willie to go for a ride one morning at dawn, even though I knew he was afraid of getting in trouble. My father had already sent him to work in the fields to keep us apart, and Willie didn't want to do anything that might jeopardize him being allowed to work with the horses again.''

"Did you get caught?" Kennedy asked.

"It was worse than that. Willie rode Bethany, a spirited but fairly slow horse. I took out Cyclone—my father's prize thoroughbred stud. I had been warned against ever riding him on my own. We headed across some newly plowed fields, Cyclone hit a chuckhole, and it broke his leg.''

"Damn!" Kennedy muttered.

"There was nothing I could do to cover up what had happened, so I sent Willie for my father. The horse was in such pain, flailing and screaming, the bone sticking right through the skin. My father had no recourse but to shoot it."

"That must have been awful to go through, but it's no reason to blame yourself all these years for getting Willie in trouble. You were kids, and these things happen. And surely even your father wouldn't have kept Willie working the fields all his life just for taking a ride with his son."

"I'd give anything if that was all that had happened. But I was so damn weak, and I just couldn't bear to face my father."

Stephen grew silent. As the two men led the horses through the woods, Kennedy patiently waited for him to continue.

Almost choking with emotion, Stephen finally continued, "It—it was when Willie returned with my—my father that I decided to betray him. I don't even remember thinking about it. I just did it. I saw the anger and disappointment in my father's eyes . . . and I said it was Willie who was riding Cyclone—that he took him out without permission, and that I was going after him to bring him back. I still remember the look in Willie's eyes when I did it. He was too stunned to protest, and when he finally did, I kept up the pretense. A few days later, Willie and his family were sent to work on another plantation, and I never saw him again."

Tom Kennedy sighed. When he finally looked up at Stephen, his eyes were filled with compassion. "What you did was very wrong, but you're a different person now. It's time to forgive yourself and stop dwelling on the past."

"I can't avoid the fact that Willie and his family were uprooted because of me."

"Let me suggest something different," Kennedy said. "No matter what else your father may be, he certainly doesn't sound stupid. And no father of a twelve year old is going to believe a story like you gave him. No, it's much more likely that he knew all along that you were the guilty one. He probably took a certain amount of pride in the way you passed the blame off on a colored servant. It showed that his training was all but complete, and that you were learning what it takes to be a white master."

Stephen looked up curiously at Kennedy. "Damned if you might not be right. I've suspected the same thing all along, but I was afraid to admit it to myself."

"That's why he got rid of Willie and his family," Kennedy continued. "If he were to really punish Willie—as he would have been forced to do if the boy had been at fault—you might eventually have backed down and admitted your own guilt. This way you never had a chance to backslide and atone for what you did."

Stephen blew out a deep breath. "That's all well and good, but it doesn't change the fact that I betrayed my best friend."

"And I'm afraid you're continuing to betray him." Seeing Stephen's questioning look, Kennedy added, "You betray him by letting your father win. That's what the game is all about, and every time you go against your own instincts and act the way your father wants, he wins again. Hell, I've seen it over and over since we've met. There's a real good side to you, but whenever it tries to come out, you kick it down and put on an air of bravado—as if that's what it takes to be a man." Kennedy halted and turned to the young southerner. "You know, I'm not Willie. But I could be your friend."

Stephen stared at the black man, his eyes misting. Then he hesitantly held out his hands, and the two men clasped each other's forearms.

*   *   *

It was warm and the sky was bright as Stephen and Kennedy emerged from the woods and followed the stage road south to the coach. As they approached, they could see a flurry of activity around the vehicle as Rebecca and Merrilee walked to and from a small fire that had been built nearby.

"Stephen!" Merrilee shouted as she saw her husband. She dropped the bag she was carrying and went running over to him. Stephen leaped off his horse and swept her into his arms.

"Hello, Tom!" Rebecca called, waving at her friend as she walked over. "Did you find—?"

Just then Rebecca saw the body across the back of the second horse. Kennedy had already dismounted and began now to untie the body.

"He's dead," Kennedy said as Rebecca came up alongside him. "We'll bury him with his wife." Kennedy hoisted the body over his shoulder and headed toward the coach.

"We're about to cook up some food," Merrilee told her husband. "And Laurel is back."

"Great," Stephen said as he put his arm around her and led the horses over to the coach. "Is Quint's boy all right?"

"Lucas is fine. But Quint . . ."

"What's wrong?" Stephen quickly asked in concern.

"He's in the coach. He ran into a pack of wild dogs, and they cut him up pretty badly before he was able to drive them off. Laurel and Lucas found him, and they brought him back on a sled. Laurel just finished stitching the worst of his wounds."

"Amazing," Stephen said as he saw the makeshift sled leaning against the side of the coach.

Reaching the stagecoach, he tied the horses to the tongue and followed his wife to the open door. Inside, Quint was propped up on the rear bench, his legs carefully

wrapped in bandages, a huge smile on his face. Laurel and
Lucas sat beside him on the center bench, with Little Bear
wagging his tail in the aisle.

"Nice to see you boys made it back all right," Quint
said as Stephen and Kennedy peered in at him. "I trust
you had more luck getting horses than I did?"

"They're up front, and they're fine," Stephen told
him. "But how are you?"

Quint reached over and took Laurel's hand. "With a
nurse—excuse me—a doctor like Laurel, I'm nearly back
to normal." He turned to look at her and said with
genuine affection, "You make quite a seamstress, Laurel."

The next few hours were spent preparing a hot meal
and readying the stagecoach for travel. The final task was to
dig a pair of graves for Sadie and Arvis Goode, who were
laid to rest beside the stage road under the pines. Laurel
decided, however, that Josiah's body would be brought to
Durango for burial.

With Quint listening from inside the coach, Rebecca
spoke a few words over the graves. Then Stephen went to
check the harness while the other passengers boarded.

When Stephen reappeared in the doorway, Quint asked,
"Well, boys, how about hoisting me up into the box so we
can get this vehicle rolling?"

"No, Quint, I cannot allow that," Laurel said firmly.

"What do you mean? You *do* want to get to Durango,
and from the way that snow is melting, we better start
moving before the Animas River becomes too high to
cross."

"Okay, but not with you driving."

"My legs are fine," Quint insisted. "They feel like
new."

"I'm not taking any chance on you breaking open
those stitches," Laurel replied. "Someone else will have
to drive."

"But this is no buckboard," Quint pointed out. "It's a team of four."

Tom Kennedy leaned forward and placed a hand on Quint's arm. "Seems to me we've got someone on board who can handle the job." Stephen Davis blushed slightly as Kennedy nodded toward him and said, "That's the man for you, Quint. I've seen him handle those horses, and I, for one, would feel more than comfortable in his hands."

Quint looked at the two men, trying to read beyond Kennedy's words. Finally he smiled and said, "Well, from what you've told me, we wouldn't even have the horses if not for Stephen, so it sounds like he's the man for the job. What do you say, Mr. Davis?"

Stephen glanced at each of the passengers, then replied, "I'll give it my best, Quint."

"Good. And I'll be right up there beside you to—"

"I'm sorry, Quint," cut in Laurel, "but I want you to stay inside the coach."

"I'll be glad to help up top," Kennedy put in.

"Yes," Stephen agreed. "We'll handle it just fine."

Quint threw up his hands and shrugged. "Looks like I'm outnumbered. Oh, well, I've always wanted to see what it feels like to get hauled around like royalty in one of these contraptions." He leaned over and gave his son a playful hug.

It took three hours for the stagecoach to come down out of the wooded hills to the banks of the Animas River. It was midafternoon, and the temperature had soared into the sixties. The snow was melting as rapidly as it had fallen, and as the coach neared the riverbank, the passengers could hear the roar of the swollen river.

Quint leaned around and stuck his head out the window. Even before he could see the Animas, he knew the situation was serious.

"Pull up well before the river!" he shouted up to the

driver's box. "Don't try to cross until we check things out!"

Stephen was already pulling back on the reins, and the stagecoach shuddered to a halt. "Damn! Look at that river roll!" he called out.

The doors flew open and Little Bear leaped out, followed by Lucas and Merrilee. Laurel and Rebecca helped steady Quint as he emerged, having insisted on seeing the situation firsthand.

Tom Kennedy climbed down from the box and helped Quint over to a large boulder beside the road. "What do you think?" he asked as Quint sat down and surveyed the scene.

Upstream, the river was a raging torrent that churned over huge, barely submerged rocks. Directly ahead, the river widened and was free of boulders, providing a normally placid crossing for horses and stagecoach. But now the water raced by in a furious sweep, rumbling into the neck of a narrower channel downstream where the rapids resumed.

"It usually only gets like this in the spring," Quint said, his voice subdued.

"Is all this from the snowmelt?" Stephen asked, coming over to where the passengers were gathered.

"That's part of it," Quint said, "but it looks like much of the area just got rain last night. The water's got to go somewhere."

"What will we do?" Laurel asked.

"We can wait, or we can cross."

"Could we make it?" Rebecca asked.

Quint looked upstream a moment, then turned to the others. "It really isn't any worse than most of the spring crossings I've made. See how wide the river is ahead? That's because it is so shallow. It's the speed of the water that causes the danger—that and the chance the horses might panic. Of course, one of us could take a horse across and get assistance from the next station—it's just a few miles beyond the river. But I'm afraid that by the time help arrives, the level will have risen even higher, and a crossing will be impossible.''

"Then let's cross right now," Stephen said with enthusiasm. "After all, we've been through so much already that it'd be a damn shame to have to go for help at the last obstacle."

"I feel the same way," Rebecca agreed. Laurel and Kennedy nodded, as well.

"Then let's give it a try!" Quint turned to Laurel. "One condition, however. I'm not staying inside the coach—I'm going to be up on the box." He noted a slight look of disappointment in Stephen's eyes and added, "Our young driver, here, will need expert advice if he is going to take us across."

Stephen's expression lit with pride.

"Agreed," Laurel said, "As long as Tom rides up there beside you to make sure you don't go for a swim!"

Quint chuckled, then stood up shakily and said, "Well, folks, let's get started!"

A few minutes later, everyone was back on board. Inside, Lucas and the women huddled against the upstream side of the stagecoach, as Quint had instructed, so that their weight would help overcome the force of the river trying to topple them downstream. Little Bear alone commanded the downstream windows, and he barked playfully at the thundering current. Up on the driver's seat, Stephen rode on the upstream side, with Quint in the middle working the bullwhip and Kennedy to Quint's right.

As Stephen laced the reins through his fingers, Quint placed a restraining hand on his arm.

"Not just yet, Stephen," he cautioned. "Let's be clear on what's going to happen. Things should be fine as long as the coach keeps moving. We don't want to give the horses a chance to get frightened. An equal danger is that the coach will stop completely and start to sink into the silty bottom. But the wheels are big, and that won't happen unless we stop moving. So no matter what, keep the horses going."

"I will," Stephen replied, lifting the reins to slap them against the horses' backs.

Again Quint held him back. "One more thing," he said, waiting until Stephen looked at him. "I don't care what Laurel said. If there is any trouble—if you get at all worried—just give me the reins. I'm plenty fit enough to handle things in an emergency."

Stephen nodded, and as Quint let go of his arm, he raised the reins and brought them down hard with a sharp "Hee yah!"

At once the stagecoach lurched forward and began to rumble down the embankment. The horses seemed hesitant to enter the water, but when Quint snapped the whip above their heads, they immediately leaped forward into the churning river.

As the stagecoach followed, Quint turned to Tom Kennedy and shouted above the roar, "How high up the wheel is the water?"

Kennedy leaned over the side, then reported, "It's just topping the hubs."

Quint looked concerned but kept his silence.

"Yah! Yah!" Stephen yelled as the coach continued toward the center of the waterway.

There was a sudden lurching crash on the upstream side, and Quint leaned behind Stephen and peered over the edge of the roof. "Just a floating log," he called out as he sat back up. What he did not tell them was that the water was now beginning to pound the bottom panels of the carriage body. If it got much higher, the pressure could easily tip the vehicle over.

The horses began to falter as the force of the river beating against the coach created an added drag. "Keep 'em moving!'' Quint exhorted as he raised the bullwhip and snapped it over their heads. "Can't bog down here!"

With a flurry of shouts and the constant cracking of Quint's whip, Stephen managed to keep the stage moving out into the center of the current. Suddenly the air was pierced by a voice shrieking, *"Quint! The horses!"*

Simultaneously, the three men looked upstream beyond the stage team and saw a gigantic tree limb floating down the river directly at the horses. It was impossible to back away, so Stephen slapped the reins and urged the horses forward, hoping to outrun the battering ram.

The men watched helplessly as the huge limb hit a rock, rolled sideways, and careened broadside into the lead horse. As the limb twirled in place and banged against him, the animal reared up, and the stagecoach came to a jarring halt. The current now spun the limb around the back of the horse. One end went under the tongue of the stage and the other flipped up, until the limb was jammed nearly upright against the tongue between the lead and rear horses.

"Hold them steady!" Quint shouted. "If they move, they could break their legs!"

The horses whinnied in fear, but Stephen's firm hands and voice kept them from totally succumbing to their panic.

Tom Kennedy was already up off the bench. Throwing his feet over the front of the box, he lowered himself into the water above the tongue of the coach. Quint dropped the whip and kneeled painfully on the floor of the driver's box. He grabbed Kennedy's wrists to steady him as he sought a footing on the tongue.

"I've got it!" Kennedy shouted, and Quint cautiously released his wrists.

The water swirled up around his knees as Kennedy turned in place and reached for the harness on the back of the right rear horse. Getting a firm grip, he let go of the coach and pulled himself up between the rear horses. Hanging on to their harnesses, he made his way forward, until he was even with their necks.

"Easy, fellas!" he shouted as they snorted and tossed their heads in fear.

Kennedy tried to kick the limb free, but it would not budge. Finally he moved up alongside the limb, let go of the right horse, and grabbed hold of the end that was sticking upright out of the water. Trying to keep his grip on the left horse with his other hand, he fought the pressure of the river as he struggled to push the limb upstream away from the tongue. It slowly bent back, until all at once the bottom slid under the tongue and the entire limb disappeared under the surface of the river.

Kennedy let go just in time, but had to frantically grab the bridle to keep from tumbling into the water. As he steadied himself and turned around, he saw the huge limb reappear downstream beyond the stage team.

Kennedy looked up at the driver's box and saw that Quint was signaling him to return, but he shook his head and turned around. Carefully he made his way out along the tongue, past the rear horses and up beside the lead pair. Standing there between the horses, he turned back to the box and waved for Stephen to start them up again.

Stephen looked at Quint, who nodded, so Stephen slapped the reins and shouted the animals forward. But they did not respond. He tried again and again, but in their fear the animals refused to budge.

Tom Kennedy walked out to the end of the tongue and grabbed hold of the bit of the upstream horse. Then he lowered himself to the river bottom. The water raged around him, foaming up against his chest, as he found his footing and pulled at the bit, urging the horse forward. The animal whinnied, tried to fight the bit, then began to move. The others followed, and slowly the stagecoach began to lift up out of the silt into which it had begun to sink.

As he prepared to climb back onto the tongue, Kennedy glanced upstream and saw that a huge mass of twisted logs and branches was floating directly toward the lead horse. Determined to forestall another catastrophe, Kennedy moved upstream beside the horse, braced himself, let go of the bit with his right hand, and turned to ward off the oncoming debris.

Kennedy threw all his weight against the onrushing mass, diverting it around the horses. But in taking the brunt of the impact head on, he was struck on the side of the face by a heavy branch that protruded from the pile. Kennedy lost his grip on the horse and was immediately swept downstream, his body caught amid the tangled debris.

"Tom!" Stephen Davis shouted in despair. He quickly handed the reins to Quint and jumped to his feet. With only a brief glance back at Quint, he leaped over the side of the coach and dove into the churning waters below.

With powerful strokes, Stephen swam toward the floating mass in the distance. He could already sense the change in the current as the river channel narrowed ahead—and he knew he would not overtake Kennedy before they entered the rapids below.

The water began to boil around him. Stephen tried to relax his body and ride over the hidden boulders, but time and again he felt his arms and legs smash against stone. He started to go under and managed to catch his breath, then reemerged long enough to gasp again before going back under.

Stephen was choking and sputtering as his head came up again. He felt as though he were racing out of control down a winding chute, helpless to do anything but hold his breath and pray. Then out of nowhere, a wall of brambles reared up in front of him, and he went crashing into it. It was like being pierced by a dozen lances at once, and he almost passed out with the pain.

Clutching for something to grab onto so that he would not be sucked back under, Stephen realized he had struck a mass of branches, which had jammed among the rocks like a dam.

"Tom!" he tried to call, but his words were garbled with water. Hanging on to the branches, he pulled himself around to the side. "Tom!" he called again, then felt his hand grab a handful of hair under the water.

Stephen reached down and pulled Tom Kennedy to the surface. He had no idea whether Kennedy was unconscious or dead, but he knew he had to get them out of the river. Looking around him, Stephen saw that the water to the left was far less furious than it was to the right. He wrapped his arm around the black man's chest, careful to keep his head above water, and slowly pulled them along the mass of branches toward shore.

There was a ten-foot gap between the end of the debris and shore. Without hesitating, Stephen gripped Kennedy tighter, held his breath, and pushed off into the current. The rapids immediately caught them up and carried them downstream. But Stephen fought to angle them toward shore, and slowly he brought them into the gentler flow at the water's edge.

Stephen found his footing and pulled Kennedy up onto the bank. Laying him out on his back, Stephen turned his head to the side and began alternately to press on his chest and slap his cheeks.

"You're not gonna die, Tom!" he shouted. "I won't let you die!"

Quint Burgess had been able to get the horses moving again after Stephen dove into the water. A few minutes later he drove the stagecoach up onto the northern bank of the Animas River.

Before the coach had come to a halt, one of the doors flew open and Merrilee leaped out. She had seen her husband dive into the water, and she was hysterical with fright as she went running downstream along the river. Laurel jumped out and soon caught up to her, but Merrilee pulled free and continued downstream, sobbing as she stumbled along. Running up alongside the distraught young woman, Laurel put an arm around her shoulders and spoke soothingly to her as they headed downriver together.

There were no trees on this side of the Animas River, so Quint drove the stage off the road and followed after the women. The procession continued for nearly a half mile without any sign of the two men, and Quint was just about to give up hope when he heard an unusual sound in the distance.

As the stagecoach approached, Quint made out curious snatches of music being sung by two horribly off-key voices. Just then Stephen Davis and Tom Kennedy appeared from around the bend, walking arm in arm as their discordant voices clashed in a simultaneous rendition of "Dixie" and "The Battle Hymn of the Republic."

Seeing her husband waving at her, Merrilee broke down in tears. Then she found herself crying with laughter as she went racing into his arms.

Chapter Eleven

The light was beginning to fade as the stagecoach approached Animas Station, a weather-beaten cluster of wooden buildings with a dilapidated rail fence delineating the yard. The station sat in a barren, windswept field, with the Rocky Mountains forming an impressive backdrop in the early evening haze.

Stephen Davis and Tom Kennedy sat alone in the driver's box, with Quint Burgess resting comfortably below. Sighting the station, Kennedy commented, "It looks deserted."

"We're almost a day late. They may not be expecting us. Quint said they might figure we stayed in Farmington to wait out the storm."

"The gate is open," Kennedy said, pointing at an opening in the fence. "Might as well pull right in."

Just then the front door of the way station creaked open and a gaunt little woman stepped out onto the porch. Shielding her eyes against the setting sun, she stared at the stagecoach for a moment, then waved her arm to signal it in.

"Not much of a welcome," Stephen said.

"The stationmaster's probably too busy eating supper to pay any attention to a coach fool enough to tempt that storm," Kennedy replied.

Stephen turned the stagecoach in a wide arc that

brought it in front of the main building. He pulled back on the reins, bringing the coach to a graceful stop, then leaped from the driver's box and called out with a flourish, "Animas Station! Last stop before the next stop!"

Kennedy climbed down as Stephen helped the women from the coach. Then the two men helped Quint down the iron steps to the ground.

Seeing the questioning expression of the woman who stood alone by the open door of the station, Quint called out, "Hello, Bertha. I had a little accident—nothing serious. Where's Ed?"

"Uh, he got to worrying and rode into Durango to see if they had a wire from Farmington."

"That's okay," Quint replied. "These hardy gents would be pleased to hitch up a new team. Any chance on a little food first?"

"Sure, Quint. It's right inside," Bertha said as she disappeared into the shadowed interior.

The women mounted the porch and entered the cabin first, followed by Stephen and Kennedy, supporting Quint between them. Lucas stayed behind a moment, patting Little Bear, but as the three men crossed the threshold, he went racing up the stairs and rushed inside. Little Bear came bounding behind him, but the door closed abruptly in his face, leaving the big black dog feebly whining and scratching to be let in.

"Hello, folks!" a reedy voice sang out as the door slammed shut behind the travelers. They spun around to see a haggard-looking little man leaning on a crutch. His big, unkempt partner stood grinning beside him.

"So nice of you to come," Ned Purvis continued. "Custer and I have looked forward to seeing you again."

"We sure have," Custer Vance said as he waggled his revolver at them.

"Sorry the stationmaster couldn't greet you himself," Purvis said. "At the moment he's sort of all tied up out back.'' Raising his own revolver, Purvis turned to his partner. ''Check for weapons.''

Vance hurried forward and quickly confirmed everyone was unarmed.

''Okay, everybody over by those chairs,'' Purvis ordered as he hobbled across the room on his crutch. His pantleg was stained with blood where Sadie Goode had shot him.

''What happened to the rest of you?'' Purvis asked as Vance pushed each of the passengers into the chairs that had been set up along one wall. ''There was an older couple, and that fool old doctor.''

''You killed him,'' Laurel said, glaring at him.

''That's tough luck. He should have listened. And the others?''

''Dead, too,'' Quint said. ''Froze in the storm.''

Custer Vance began to chuckle, but Purvis silenced him with a sharp look. ''Tie and gag them,'' he ordered, tossing Vance some rope and cloth that was laid out on the dining table.

One by one, Vance tied Quint, Lucas, the passengers, and the stationmaster's wife to the chairs, then crudely gagged each one with a strip of cloth. As soon as he was finished, Ned Purvis placed his revolver on the table and approached the line of chairs.

''Looks like we're gonna get a chance to finish what we started, Custer,'' he said with a leer.

Stopping in front of Merrilee, Purvis reached out and tore open the collar of her dress. ''Not bad, huh? You like this one, Custer?''

Two chairs away, Stephen tried to shout and struggled to free himself.

Purvis hobbled over to him and said, ''She your woman? Then when it comes her turn, maybe we'll let you watch.''

Next to Stephen, Tom Kennedy stared impassively forward as Ned Purvis stepped in front of him.

"What about you, nigra boy? You got a woman here?"

When Kennedy did not respond, Purvis slapped him full force across the cheek. Kennedy's head reeled back, but when he looked up at Purvis, his eyes held the same impassive expression.

"I bet you wish you had one of these women, nigra boy, or are you too good for our white women? Maybe you prefer heathen meat." He slapped him again, then started to chuckle.

Spinning on his crutch, Ned Purvis moved up the line to where Laurel was seated. He leaned forward until his face was only a few inches from hers.

"We're gonna have a real nice party, half-breed, and you're gonna be the first one to show us a good time. Ain't that nice? It ought to be, because at least you won't have to see what happens to the rest of your friends. You'll be the first one to die!"

Purvis broke into a belly laugh as he waved Custer Vance over.

"Untie her," he ordered, then stepped back to the table and picked up his revolver.

After the rope was removed, Vance started to reach for the gag, but Purvis called out, "Leave it on. I don't need to listen to some damn uncivilized heathen squaw. Anyway, all she needs to do is moan, and she can do that just fine gagged."

Vance pulled Laurel roughly to her feet.

"Want the first turn?" Purvis offered.

Vance merely grinned and began to drag her toward a half-closed door across the room. When Laurel held back, Vance roughly twisted her arm behind her back. He kicked open the door and pushed her into the bedroom beyond.

As the door slammed shut, Purvis stared down the line of people, then suddenly turned toward the bedroom and called out, "Not yet, Custer. There's somebody who wants to watch."

Purvis made his way over to the chair on which Lucas was tied. He quickly removed the rope and hauled the boy to his feet.

"The innocent little idiot boy needs an education," he called back to the prisoners as he dragged Lucas to the bedroom.

Purvis thrust the bedroom door open wide so that Lucas and everyone in the cabin could see what was going on inside. Custer Vance had already thrown Laurel onto the bed, and he leaned over now and ripped open her buckskin blouse. Laurel tried to crawl away, but Vance slammed the side of her head with his fist and dragged her back toward him.

Purvis held Lucas by the shoulders. Seeing that the boy was turning away, he grabbed his hair and yanked his head around. "Look, boy!" he shouted. "And if you're real good, I might even give you a turn!"

Lucas began to moan, his teeth clamped down on the cloth gag. He tried to turn away as the big, slovenly man started to pull up Laurel's skirt, but the man with the crutch twisted his head to force him to look. When he shut his eyes, the man smacked his face.

Lucas could bear it no longer. He raised his right foot and kicked back as hard as he could against the outlaw's wounded leg. The man shrieked and doubled over, releasing his hold on the boy. Lucas quickly clasped his hands together and jabbed his elbow back, catching the man squarely on the nose and knocking him to the ground.

Custer Vance had just begun to remove his trousers when he heard his partner scream and go sprawling across the floor. He forgot about Laurel and leaped to his feet, his trousers slipping to his ankles but his long johns still in place. Yanking up his pants, he started across the room but found himself facing Ned Purvis's revolver. Young Lucas Burgess held it pointed right at his belly.

"N-now don't d-do that!" Vance pleaded as the boy gritted his teeth and began to squeeze the trigger.

Lucas's hands were shaking as he summoned the will to shoot. Images of Laurel's dead father flooded his brain, and he yearned to make this man bleed the same way.

"D-don't d-do it!" Vance stammered.

Lowering her dress, Laurel slid to the edge of the bed and wrapped her torn blouse around her. She pulled away the gag as she stood and slowly approached Lucas.

"Don't shoot," she calmly told the boy. "I am fine." She nodded and smiled at Lucas.

The boy's hands wavered. He looked at Laurel, then back at the fat outlaw. His expression darkened, and again he struggled to squeeze the trigger.

"I am fine," Laurel kept repeating as she slowly stepped in front of Custer Vance.

Suddenly Lucas realized he was pointing the weapon at Laurel. His hands relaxed, and he began to lower the gun.

Laurel quickly stepped forward and took it from him. She turned and trained it on Vance.

"Pick him up!" she ordered, pointing at Ned Purvis.

Throwing his hands up and nodding that he would do as she said, Vance hurried over to where his partner was struggling to his knees. He hauled Purvis to his feet and dragged him across the main room.

Laurel turned to Lucas. "Untie the others," she said. "Get Quint."

Lucas immediately understood and ran over to release his father.

Vance dumped Ned Purvis in a chair at the table, then began to button his own trousers. Just then Lucas released Quint, who quickly tore off his gag and stormed across the room, unmindful of the searing pain in his legs. Before Vance could react, Quint grabbed him by the collar and unleashed a devastating right cross against the big man's jaw.

As Vance crumpled to the floor, Quint leaped upon

him, striking him again and again, then lifting his head and pounding it against the floorboards. He felt someone tugging at his shoulders, and he spun around, ready to strike out, but found himself facing Laurel.

"No more!" Laurel shouted, pulling at his arm. "Please! No more!"

Spinning back around, Quint pulled his arm free and lifted it to strike Vance again.

"You're doing this for yourself, not me!" she shouted as she held onto his arm and deflected his blow away from the half-conscious outlaw. Again and again she pulled at Quint, until he began to relax and turned back to look at her.

As Laurel threw her arms around Quint's neck and hugged him, she whispered, "Let the violence be theirs, not ours. Never ours!"

Quint let go of Custer Vance, and the big man fell back against the floor. Then Quint turned, wrapped his arms around Laurel, and held her close.

By now Lucas had freed the other passengers. With a broad grin, Tom Kennedy crossed the room and yanked a terrified Ned Purvis to his feet.

Twisting Purvis's collar and turning him to face Laurel, Kennedy said, "You're one lucky white boy. If it weren't for that *uncivilized heathen squaw*, you'd be dead right now!"

Kennedy stared a moment at the squirming little man, then sighed as he said, "Oh, hell, ain't nobody ever accused this *nigra boy* of being civilized!" With that he held Ned Purvis at arm's length, pulled back his other fist, and sent it crashing into Purvis's already battered nose.

Two days later, the passengers from the Durango Overland Stage Line gathered at a small cemetery outside Durango, Colorado.

Quint Burgess and his son together held the shovel as they scooped up some dirt and tossed it down onto the casket below. "Good-bye, Josiah Fox," Quint said. "And thank you." Seated nearby, Little Bear looked up and barked once, then rested his head back on his paws.

Tom Kennedy came forward now, tears misting his eyes. He took the shovel from Lucas, quickly dug into the loose pile of dirt beside the open grave, and added another shovelful. He handed the shovel to Rebecca Williman, who repeated the process. Merrilee Davis stepped forward next, and then her husband.

Finally Laurel Fox approached the grave and took the shovel from Stephen. She dumped one and then another shovelful of dirt into the grave, working silently until the pile was gone and the hole was filled. Then she handed the shovel to Quint and kneeled down upon the loose mound of earth. She scooped some dirt into each hand and let it pour between her fingers back to the grave.

"He'e'e' Ahi'ni'yo'," she softly intoned as Quint came up behind her and placed his hands on her shoulders. "Walk with the Spirit." Then she reached up and took Quint's hands in her own.

After another moment of silence, Laurel stood and walked arm in arm with Quint to where their friends were gathered. Lucas hurried forward, and she wrapped her other arm around his shoulder.

"Isn't it time for your train?" Laurel asked Merrilee Davis.

"Don't worry, we have plenty of time," Merrilee assured her.

"You're headed straight to Georgia?" Quint asked.

Stephen grinned. "I think we've had enough excitement for one honeymoon. Anyway, there are things we need to clear up . . ." He glanced at his wife, and she nodded for him to continue. ". . . Before we leave again."

"Leave?" Laurel asked. "Where are you going?"

"Merrilee and I have given it a lot of thought, and we've decided that we like this new frontier out here.

We're determined to come west and start our own horse ranch. We'll succeed or fail on our own terms."

"That's wonderful," Quint said.

Looking at Tom Kennedy, Stephen continued, "I have a good friend named Willie Adams who is particularly good with horses. I thought I might look him up and offer him a job—if he'd like to try a new life."

As Kennedy smiled, Merrilee took hold of her husband's arm, her face beaming with pride. "Stephen isn't just going to raise horses, either. He's promised to take up painting again."

"There's a wealth of material out here, and damn few painters," Stephen noted.

Tom Kennedy walked over to a nearby buggy, which he and Rebecca had driven to the cemetery. As he returned, he was carrying a wooden box.

"Stephen," he said, "perhaps this will be of some use to you." He held out the box, and when Stephen hesitated, he added, "Go on, it's for you."

Accepting the box, Stephen opened the clasps and raised the lid. Inside was a set of oil paints and brushes.

"Tom, I can't—"

"Oh, yes, you can," Kennedy cut in. "And furthermore, I expect you to send one of your paintings to Santa Fe for us to hang at Williman Mining over Miss Rebecca's desk."

"You're going back, then?" Laurel asked Rebecca.

"Of course. Someone has to run the company, and I think I can handle the job as well as any man."

"Better," Kennedy put in.

"Maybe, with your help."

"I take it you'll be staying with Williman Mining," Stephen said to Kennedy.

"As long as Williman Mining will have me," Kennedy replied. "And there's someone else I hope will have me—Abigail. I've been a damn fool for too long. I'm determined to make her my wife, if she can find it in her to forgive me."

Stephen clapped his friend on the back. "After all you've taught me about forgiveness, I'm sure you'll have no trouble gaining it yourself." Stephen then turned to Quint and asked, "What about you and Lucas? Will you continue with the stage line?"

"Not after the next run. I've given notice. It was about time for a change."

"What will you do?" Merrilee asked.

"Since we arrived in Durango, Laurel has had a chance to properly examine my son's condition, and she's quite certain his entire problem is his hearing—that it has nothing to do with his intelligence."

"Yes," Laurel agreed, "and I'm not convinced it is untreatable. Back east there is some remarkable work being done by Alexander Graham Bell and his associates, and I would like them to take a look at Lucas. Even if his hearing cannot be helped, there are new methods of teaching the deaf that we will pursue."

"Why, Laurel even thinks that Lucas is far more intelligent than most children his age," Quint said with pride. "She has discovered that somehow he has taught himself to read lips. And remember the way he helped her during that operation? Who knows—maybe with enough book learning he'll be accepted someday by one of those eastern medical schools!"

"But only if it's his dream and not just yours," Laurel playfully teased, and everyone laughed.

"Then you won't be returning just yet to the Ute reservation, Laurel?" Merrilee asked.

Rebecca turned to Merrilee and announced, "Laurel has decided to enter medical school after all."

"As I told Rebecca yesterday, I have made a most unexpected discovery," Laurel explained. "Now that my father has released me from the obligation to be licensed as a physician, I have discovered that it is something I want to do. You see, I always knew that the Ute people do not care whether or not I have such a piece of paper. But my dream is not to merely serve my mother's people, but to help bridge her world and my father's. And as a licensed physician, I will be taken far more seriously by my father's people.''

''Do you think you'll be able to gain admission to a medical school?'' Stephen asked.

''I still have my father's letters of introduction to Geneva Medical College, and Rebecca has been kind enough to offer to write her own letter of recommendation to the college.''

''And while we're back east,'' Quint said, ''we intend to see what we can do about changing our government's Indian policy, so that maybe the Southern Ute and other tribes can remain on their own land.''

''I'll be doing what I can from this end,'' Rebecca promised. ''Williman Mining is quite influential in these parts, and we'll see what we can do to make sure the Ute will not be forced from their homes.''

Stephen glanced at his pocket watch. ''We really must be going,'' he said as he ushered his wife to their rented buggy.

Quint, Laurel, and Lucas walked over to the waiting buggies, while Little Bear ran back and forth, barking playfully. Good-byes were said, and then Rebecca and Kennedy boarded one buggy and the Davises another. With a final wave, the two men slapped their reins and the buggies pulled away, Lucas and Little Bear racing after them.

As they headed down the hillside toward Durango, Tom Kennedy turned to Rebecca and asked, ''Do you really think that medical school will accept a woman? An Indian woman, no less?''

''Tom,'' Rebecca replied, ''after that letter I sent this

morning, they damn well better. You know I've always been a realist. I decided that if a recommendation from the owner of Williman Mining isn't enough to do the trick, perhaps they'll be swayed by the ten thousand dollar endowment I offered.''

Tom's mouth dropped open. "She doesn't know?"

"And she never will." With that Rebecca began to giggle.

"You shameless devil!" Tom Kennedy said, bursting into laughter.

Meanwhile, in the buggy behind, Merrilee looked back at the couple standing beside Josiah Fox's grave and said, "Do you think Quint will ask Laurel to marry him? They would make such a lovely family."

"Didn't you notice?" Stephen asked.

"Notice what?"

"Her hand. She was wearing a ring, and it wasn't there two days ago."

"You mean, they're engaged?" Merrilee asked incredulously.

"Precisely."

Merrilee leaned over and gave her husband a passionate hug. "I only hope they are as happy as you and I!"

Back at the cemetery, Laurel lifted her hand to look at the engagement ring Quint had given her. "It is so beautiful," she said.

"Only half as beautiful as you," Quint replied as he took her in his arms and pulled her close.

Just then, Lucas and Little Bear came bounding back up the hill. The boy halted abruptly and stood some distance away, watching as his father kissed the Indian woman with the long, silver-streaked hair. Remembering his mother, whom he had loved so dearly and had lost, Lucas stooped down and wrapped his arms around Little Bear, shutting his eyes against a flood of tears.

"*Lucas . . .*"

A sweet sound played through his mind, and for a moment he thought it was the voice of his mother.

"Lucas . . ."

The gentle voice grew clearer, and he realized someone was calling his name. He opened his eyes and saw the beautiful Indian woman kneeling in front of him.

"I love you," the woman said, reaching out to him. Understanding her words, Lucas pulled back and began to cry softly.

"I love you. And I won't leave you." Laurel pulled her hair to one side and unfastened the leather thong around her neck. "I'll never leave you," she repeated as she removed her mother's amulet and held it to Lucas.

As Lucas stared at the beaded yellow sunburst, he could see Josiah Fox smiling at him. It was as though the kind old man was not gone forever, but was merely waiting to be reunited with them one day.

Looking back up, Lucas saw Laurel smiling at him. And as she again whispered, "I love you," he could see his mother mirrored in her eyes.

Lifting his hands, Lucas stammered, "M-M-Mama!" and went rushing into Laurel's arms.

Quint came over and kneeled beside Laurel and Lucas, wrapping his arms around them. As Lucas leaned up and kissed his father's cheek, Little Bear nuzzled his way into the middle and began licking their faces.

"Easy boy!" Quint shouted as the excited dog leaped up playfully and knocked him off balance. He landed on his back with a thud.

As Quint raised himself up on his elbows and grinned sheepishly, Little Bear started to bark and dance around in circles, while Laurel and Lucas clapped their hands and laughed with delight.

STAGECOACH STATION 18:

CASA GRANDE
by Hank Mitchum

Troubles seem to plague the Dundee Transport Line in 1881. The Arizona Territory stage line is overextended and underfunded, and creditors are pressing for payment. But despite all their difficulties, stage-line owner Cooper Dundee and his wife Regan are eagerly awaiting the birth of their first child.

Short on drivers, Cooper himself undertakes the stage run from Phoenix to Prescott. Waiting for him at one of the way stations is Adam Babcock, a disgruntled former employee who has managed to become rehired under an assumed identity. Babcock loosens one of the coach wheels, resulting in a crash that kills two passengers and gravely injures Cooper. Babcock, who is the first to arrive upon the scene, sees to it that Cooper is wrongly blamed for the accident by pouring liquor all over his clothing and making it look like he was drunk on the job.

As Cooper fights to prove his innocence, a mysterious businessman arrives in Phoenix, intent on taking not only Cooper's life, but also his wife's. As he ensnares other members of Cooper's family into his secret plan, Cooper is forced into an uneasy truce with his estranged brother—a truce that culminates on the stage road to Casa Grande, yielding both tragic death and the miracle of new life.